SUPERFLIRT

HELEN
CAVANAGH

SCHOLASTIC BOOK SERVICES

New York Toronto London Auckland Sydney Tokyo

For my supersister,
Alice Marie Farrenkopf
who always knows what I mean.

ISBN 0-590-30951-X

12 11 10 9 8 7 6 5 4 3 2 1   9   0 1 2 3 4 5/8

Printed in the U. S. A.   06

SUPERFLIRT

A Wildfire Book

PROLOGUE

Until this year Saturday used to be my favorite day; Sunday too. At school every Friday during last period, I was always unbearably restless, unable to sit still. I gazed out the window, fiddled with my ring, watched the hands inch slowly forward on the big round clock above the door. By the time the dismissal bell rang at two-forty, I'd feel like I imagine Mrs. Pulaski's parakeet feels when she is let out of her cage.

"Katya, dahling," she tells the small blue-green bird in her husky, heavily accented voice, "you fly free now while Mama scrubs your cage."

Mrs. Pulaski looks at Katya with great love and pride.

"Then be good girl — come back and take your bath. Get all bee-yoo-tee-full for Papa."

Katya is always ecstatic, flutter-flying from lampshade to picture frame to curtain rod, and when I'm there, to the top of my head. I understand — I *used* to feel like that.

"Katya is pleased when you come, Susan. See how she is so pleased?"

Mrs. Pulaski smiles at Katya and me fondly, her eyes mist, and then she always comes close

1

and pats my cheek and plucks lint from my clothes. She fusses over me. It's because she loves me, and also because she is a cleaning nut. She doesn't like disorder; it makes her nervous.

The Pulaskis have been our next-door neighbors for years, even before I was born sixteen years ago. They're old — somewhere in their seventies — and they never had any children. *I* am her child, *Katya* is her child — we help to fill the emptiness. Mr. Pulaski? He could care less.

I never liked Mr. Pulaski but I've been jealous of him lately. He is a lucky man — luckier and happier than I am right now. He is freer than a bird; he has friends, no problems. He even gets his cage cleaned every day. More important, he has someone always available to smooth his feathers if they get ruffled.

Not me — not anymore. Mom is too busy walking on eggshells to have time for me. When I need to talk, her answer always seems to be: "Later, Susan, okay?" But later never comes.

For months now, her main concern is keeping the house quiet during the day so Daddy can sleep, and when he's awake, keeping him soothed until it's time for him to go to work at night. If he gets off to work "without incident" (without blowing his stack about something), Mom considers the day a success.

After years of being *overlooked* and *underpaid* (his words), Daddy was finally made foreman of the entire third shift at Schwaub-Millar. S-M is Appleby's only industry; they make rainhats, trashbags, stuff like that. Last spring, when he got the promotion and a sizeable raise, we were

2

all thrilled. But no more. Daddy comes home from work in the morning exhausted, irritable, ready to explode. He worries constantly now about bills, about taxes, about *everything*. He gets mad about every little thing. He says Mom and I don't understand "the hard realities of life." What Mom and I do understand though is that Daddy hates his job — he's miserable.

I'm really sorry about that because I love my father; I really do. But it means I can't go to him with my problems either. The expression on his face sometimes reminds me of Mr. Pulaski. It's a look that says, "Don't bother me." Worse, sometimes his expression is blank — he doesn't even see me. Susan Bond — Invisible Girl.

Beginning last year, my friends, Laura Breen, Joanie Sangerville, Sandy Bartell, and Terri Lannigan, stopped being my friends. They don't call or come over, they don't invite me anywhere afterschool or on weekends. So even to them I'm an invisible person. That's why I hate Saturdays and Sundays now. Those two days are endless, empty, boring — *torture*.

I'm not even sure what happened, why they are treating me like this. They act like I'm the Wicked Witch of the West — or is it the North? Wherever she comes from, she's *me*. Everyone *hates* me!

When Mom does find a moment to notice me, she wonders aloud whey I spend so much time around the house now, and why my room is always so clean and organized.

At least there is John. I *still* have John. If it wasn't for John Michael Anthony, I don't know what I'd do. When he's not working on weekends, I get out of my cage. If it wasn't for John, I'd be just like Katya, bobbing my head in time to old fogey music on Saturday nights, and trying not to chirp too loud.

Wonderful John, he loves me. *He* thinks I'm wonderful, gorgeous, the best thing that ever happened to him. At least that's what he *thinks*.

Oh, I don't know. Maybe I am the Wicked Witch of the West. Maybe I deserve what's happened. Or maybe — *maybe* — there is something really wrong with me. . . .

CHAPTER ONE

"Okay, I've *had* it — enough is enough!"

Mom slapped the kitchen table for emphasis, and stood up.

"I think it's about time for a SASSS. What do *you* think, Susan Bee?"

"Yes." I almost yelled the word. "Excellent idea, Mom."

If it sounds like I was eager, you're wrong; desperate is the correct word. A SASSS would cancel out the BASSS that lay just ahead — another Boring And Sad Solitary Saturday.

Did Mom know she was saving me? Probably not. Anyway, I loved her at that moment, loved the familiar gleam that had returned to her cat-green eyes, and her high-beam smile that said: *let's-have-fun*. It's been a long time since I've seen her show any spirit. Needless to say, I was glad.

A SASSS is our shorthand for A Sheila And Susan Shopping Spree, something we do fantastically well together. Shopping, we are not mother and daughter; we are one person, one mind. If there is a special gene that determines your taste in clothes, then Mom passed her gene on to me without question. All the girls I know say they hate clothes-shopping with their mothers, it always ends in an argument, frustration, hurt feelings. Not us — ever.

Besides her fashion sense, Mom has passed other genes on to me. We are both fairly tall and long-legged and we have the kind of figures clothes are made for. She lightens her already light brown hair but I don't; I let the sun do it for me. And while her eyes are the purest green, mine are the tricky kind; sometimes green, but also brown, or even blue, depending on what I wear.

Our plans made, we moved fast — quick showers, shampoos, partially damp hair simply scooped back with combs, makeup, clothes. Talk about getting our act together. We were ready in thirty minutes flat.

It felt good to leave the breakfast dishes in the sink, to step over the vacuum cleaner, and to close the door on my unmade bed. Mom was right — enough is enough!

"Great day, Susan," Mom said. "Doesn't the sun feel good?"

Even her driving was different. Hunched over the steering wheel, her foot just a bit heavier on the gas pedal, she reminded me of a race-car driver. Reckless maybe, but happier, younger.

"Mmm-mm, sun," I agreed dreamily. "I *love* it."

It was winter — February — but the mild, sunny day seemed more like April. At the same moment we sang.

"Sunshine on my shoulders makes me happy . . ."

6

See what I mean about us? At our best, we are one person, one mind.

There wasn't any discussion about *where* we were going. The mall, naturally — Ferber's our first stop. At Ferber's, they placed the clearance racks in out-of-the-way corners and alcoves, hidden, really, except to savvy shoppers like Mom and me. We almost never failed to find treasure in Ferber's Department Store — some really great stuff.

After that our conversation was a mixture of short phrases, single words, and body language. A shirt held up, an eyebrow raised, a nod of the head. "This?" "Oh, you, definitely." "Yes!" "No!" "Maybe." "Interesting, try it on."

By one-thirty we called it quits. We were happy with ourselves and *starving*.

"Bun 'n' Burger?" Mom asked.

"Great!" I said.

During lunch we reviewed our purchases. A soft, creamy pullover sweater for me, a sea-green silky shirt for Mom (just a shade darker than her eyes) corduroy jeans for me, a gray wool skirt for her, socks and two plain flannel shirts for Daddy, and one huge bottle of body lotion for us to share. It was a great haul — we were in heaven. What made it even better was that everything had been marked down to make way for the spring stock. We agreed we had done very well — and on not very much money. Another successful SASSS.

But we were both very quiet on the way home. The faint lines on Mom's forehead were deeper; I knew she was worried.

"I guess he'll be mad, huh?" I asked finally.

"What?" She had been deep in her own thoughts.

"Oh, no," she said and then added defensively, "Well, we needed these things. It's been ages . . ."

Her uncertainty told the real story; she *was* worried.

Then she hit the steering wheel with the heel of her hand. When she spoke her voice was firm again.

"Listen, Susan, don't *you* worry. I'll handle him so don't worry, okay?"

"Okay, Mom," I said, "and thanks."

Maybe Daddy would surprise us and be in a good mood today. We'd model our new outfits for him, and he'd look at us and smile and tell us how pretty we looked. (How long had it been since he had done that?) But if he saw Mom's new shirt matched her eyes, and how soft and becoming my new sweater was. . . .

No such luck. When we got home, Daddy was sitting at the kitchen table, a cup of coffee in front of him. His eyes were bleary and tired-looking, and his shoulders sagged. When he spotted the Ferber bags, he groaned, and passed his hand over his eyes.

"Sheila, what are you doing to me? How much did you spend today?"

Mom has been so patient with Daddy; I knew it had to be hard for her to keep her thoughts to herself, her temper under control. Normally, she's outspoken, even fierce in her opinions. Now her temper got the best of her.

"*Don't start*, Bill," she warned. "Susan and I

had a nice day and I won't let you spoil it. I'm a careful shopper and *you know it*." She paused, "And whether you think so or not, *I* think we *deserve* it!"

Mom's eyes were fiery emeralds, and her heels came down hard on the kitchen floor.

"You could have at least discussed it with me," Dad said. He sounded like a whiny little boy.

"*What*? And *wake* you? I wouldn't dream of it!"

There was a dangerous quality to her voice. She had said she would handle it — and she was — but maybe I could help. I fished in one of the paper bags and pulled out my new sweater, the best bargain of the day.

I held it up against me, and moved closer to Daddy. I had felt so good in the sweater when I tried it on before, softly pretty, feminine, even elegant.

"Look, Daddy," I said brightly. "Twenty-five dollars marked down to twelve. Don't you love it? Does it look nice on me?"

He barely looked at me.

"Only twelve, huh?" he said and there was no mistaking the sarcasm in his voice.

I stood staring at him for a long moment and then I turned and put the sweater back in the bag.

Mom was standing at the sink; she seemed to be looking out the window, but I knew she was struggling with her own feelings. I wanted very much to put my arms around her, tell her it was all right, that I didn't mind. Certainly I didn't want to desert her now when she needed me, but

9

at the same time I couldn't wait to get out of the kitchen, the house.

"I think I'll go for a walk," I said as casually as I could. "It's such a nice day. . . ."

Over her shoulder Mom gave me a quick look of understanding.

"Why don't you wear your new sweater, Susan? It looks beautiful on you."

"I think I will," I said, and nodded my thanks.

Daddy didn't say a word; he just sipped his coffee and stared at the wall.

Suddenly I was hungry — *starved*. And that was very strange because I had only finished lunch a half hour ago.

When I left the house I didn't plan on going to Fritzie's; I just found myself opening the door and breathing in the luscious aroma of frying hamburgers and onions.

Fritzie's is *the* place to go after school or in the evening. As a matter of fact, it is the *only* place in Appleby where kids are truly welcome. Joe and Millie Fritz are middle-aged, their own kids all grown up and married. Since they opened their small restaurant, they've become Mom and Dad — or at least friends — to every kid between the ages of thirteen and eighteen. And for their sake, because they provide a place for us to go, we really try to behave well, to keep it down to a dull roar.

One thing about Fritzie's, though: you just don't walk in and sit down all by yourself. It would be like advertising: Look, everybody — no friends!

10

So what was I doing here on a Saturday afternoon without John, without anyone? I shut the door again, and turned to go. I didn't think I could be that brave, act as if I didn't care. I *did* care.

Coming toward me fast, running, all red-faced, sweaty, and out-of-breath was Tommy Bly — *Terri Lannigan's* Tommy Bly. They've been going together for years; when you say Terri, you say Tommy, a definite pair, like shoes or gloves. Tommy, as far as I knew, had never had eyes for anyone but Terri. Everyone knew and accepted that, me too.

"Hi, Tommy," I said, smiling up at him, "Hadn't you better slow down? Isn't there such a thing as too many muscles?"

I made my eyes wide with appreciation.

"Seriously, Tommy, do you jog every day? Is that how you stay in such wonderful shape?"

"Well, yeah . . ." he said haltingly, embarrassment making him tongue-tied. "I guess. . . ."

"You're just modest, Tommy Bly," I said, "And that's good too. It's so nice when a guy looks really great but doesn't act conceited about it. I always told Terri how lucky she was to have a guy like you."

"Really? I mean, you did?"

But he was grinning now, obviously flattered, pleased. I realized it was the first time he had ever really looked at me; as I said, Terri is the only girl in his life.

Now he *was* looking. "So how have you been, Susan?" he asked as if he really cared to know. He had stretched out one long arm and was letting

11

the wall of the building hold him up. Or was he holding up the wall? Tommy is about six foot four and he must weigh at least two hundred pounds.

"I'm just fine," I said. "Or I would be if I just had a Coke or something. I'm dying of thirst. Only. . . ." I let my voice trail off wistfully.

"Only what?" he asked. "What's the matter?"

"Oh, nothing," I said. "Really. It's just that I'd feel silly sitting all by myself. It's so — well, *you* know, Tommy — it's . . . *lonesome.*"

I tilted my head and laughed. "Listen to me," I said. "I sound like a little orphan girl."

He straightened up then, and rather clumsily, took my arm.

"Come on, you poor little orphan, you. Let *me* buy you a Coke." He laughed at his own cleverness. "Besides, I'm thirsty too. I've done three point four miles so far."

I let him lead me into Fritzie's and help me into a booth.

"You really are a great guy, Tommy," I said looking deep into his eyes. "Are you always so nice to lonely, thirsty girls?"

He couldn't seem to look away. "You're really pretty, Susan," he said wonderingly, "How come I . . .?"

"How come you never noticed, you mean? Because you're in love with Terri, that's why."

"Yeahhh . . ." he said. I could see, for the moment anyway, he had some doubts about that.

"Why don't you get our Cokes," I said gently, and then added in an even softer voice, "I'll be right here. I won't go away."

"Sure — okay," he said and got up. He looked

down at me for a moment with a dazed look in his eyes. "What kind of Coke did you say you wanted, Susan?"

I knew my eyes were warm and sparkly as I looked up at him. "A *Coke* Coke, Tommy."

"Oh, yeah," he said. "Sure. . . ."

The truth was that I was a bit dazed too. How had this happened? I certainly hadn't planned it; Terri was the only girl in my old crowd who was still halfway nice to me. If she found out about this. . . .

Tommy didn't seem to be worried about it, though. He brought the Cokes back to the table and proceeded to question me about John.

"I don't see you together very often," he said. "Are you still going with him or what?"

"Sure I am," I said, and shrugged. "It's just that he works a lot — after school and on Saturdays."

I guess I put on a forlorn expression because he said, "John's a dope. A girl like you. . . ."

I gave him my very best smile. "A girl like *what*, Tommy?"

I realized I was holding my breath. This was the part I liked best.

Tommy suddenly looked uncomfortable; he bent his head and fiddled with his watch, twisting it back and forth.

"I shouldn't say it," he said. "Terri. . . ."

"Tommy," I said very softly. "I'm not going to tell Terri."

He relaxed slightly. "Yeah . . . well, I was just going to say that you're very. . . ."

I leaned in close and touched his hand very

13

lightly. "Go ahead, say it. I'm not going to *hit* you."

". . . very special," he said. "And very pretty. I like your hair. What color is it, anyway?"

I smiled and shook my hair back from my face, aware that the sunlight streaming through the plate glass window was doing good things to it.

"Oh, just brown," I said. "Dull old brown."

"No, it isn't," he said, staring at my face and hair with a kind of helpless fascination. "I see all kinds of colors in it — red, gold."

I gave him another great smile. "Tommy, you really are a great guy. I like you."

"Do you, Susan? Really?" He hesitated for just a second. "Would you ever go out with me? I mean, sometimes I wonder if maybe I'm missing something, sticking with one girl all this time. Do you ever feel that way?"

Suddenly, I was very uneasy. Why did I always get more than I bargained for? I had only meant to . . .

I shrugged. "Oh, I don't know," I said. "I guess I never really thought about it."

"Well, *think* about it, Susan," he said. "Maybe I'll call you sometime . . . maybe we can go out."

"Sure, Tommy," I said, standing up. "I'll think about it."

"Are you leaving?" he said, "I thought . . ."

"I have to get home now," I said quickly. "Thanks for the Coke. I'll see you."

It was only when I turned and headed for the door that I saw them: Laura Breen and Joanie Sangerville, sitting in a booth on the other side.

14

And, of course, they saw me too. Chances are they had been there the whole time.

Oh, great, I thought. Joanie, of all people. More than anyone else, she had it in for me. I knew, without a doubt, that Terri would hear about this, probably as soon as Joanie could get to a phone. They would have something else to hold against me. Great, just what I needed.

But when I got outside, I took a deep, deep breath, and straightened my shoulders. What had I done? Nothing terrible. Just a little harmless flirting, that's all. What was wrong with it? I liked it and Tommy certainly liked it. And it wasn't something I ever *planned* to do. It just seemed to happen. It wasn't my fault if boys liked me, liked to talk to me, thought I was special. Joanie and Laura and the rest of the girls were just jealous. That was it — jealous. So what was I supposed to do about that?

One other thing bothered me. I had been dying for a hamburger when I first got to Fritzie's, planned to order one. So how come I hadn't? I shrugged, dismissing the thought easily. No big deal. Somehow, I had just lost my appetite.

CHAPTER TWO

"May I sit with you, Susan?"

It was Terri Lannigan. I almost choked on my sandwich.

I wasn't exactly sitting alone at the long lunch-room table; four other girls and a couple of tenth-grade boys shared it with me, but they all were seated at the far end.

"Sure, Terri," I said, waving my hand to indi-cate the empty seats across from and on either side of me. "You're in luck — my fan club just left."

I said it with a bravado I didn't really feel, and also to break the ice. But it didn't work. She didn't smile, or give me an answer back. She just looked thoughtful.

That worried me, but not too much. Terri is like that, thoughtful, careful, basically a very serious girl. She does have a lighter side, almost a wild side, but it is used only in the fantastic, extravagant stories she tells and writes. Sometime around the fourth grade, Terri decided she was going to be a writer, and since then she had been working at it. At sleepover parties, we would often keep her awake half the night. On request, she could make up the greatest stories — right off the top of her head — romances, fantasies, the scary kind. She was editor of *The Core*, Appleby High's school paper, and she was very well liked. Even though she had stopped hanging around with me, I still felt she was my friend. She was the only one of my former crowd who still talked to me, walked to class with me, ate lunch with me — like now.

She looked different today, I couldn't figure out why. Her hair? No, she wore it the usual way: long, blond, wavy. Beautiful hair. I suppose I was staring at her.

"What's the matter, Susan?" she asked quietly.

"I don't know. You look different somehow. I was just. . . ."

"I *am* different," she said. "But I wasn't aware that it showed."

Suddenly I did not want to ask what she meant by that. I was very uneasy.

I guess whether I was interested or not, it didn't matter. Terri had something on her mind and she was going to say it.

"Susan, I've always been an optimist. You know that from my stories' happy endings. My dad always shakes his head at me and says, 'Don't expect so much from life, Terri. You'll be disappointed.' But Susan, I figured he was wrong, too cynical. I really believed life was good, *people* were good — that if you were decent, people would be decent to you."

She looked down at her tray, at her uneaten hamburger. She ignored that and took a sip of her chocolate milk. Then she looked at me, and I could see tears glistening in her fine gray eyes.

"Have I ever been unfair to you, Susan?" she asked. There was a quiver in her voice.

"No, of course not, Terri," I said quickly, "You've always been . . ."

She didn't let me finish. "Tommy broke up with me Saturday night."

"Oh, no, Terri," I said quickly. "That's terrible. How . . .?"

"He saw someone who he likes better, or as he said, would like to know better. *You*, Susan. He wants *you*."

I shook my head back and forth in denial. "No," I said. "No, he doesn't. He just . . ."

"Just what?" she asked quietly. "Is he just like all the others? Doesn't he understand that all you want is another conquest, another notch on your belt, or whatever? You do such a great job of it, Susan. I guess I have to give you credit. Tommy came over Saturday night and he felt ten feet tall. I thought he was just in a very good mood, until he started talking about how he thought we were in a rut, that we should see what it's like to go out with someone else once in a while. He said . . . he felt . . . tied down."

I thought of Joanie Sangerville. Who did Terri think she was kidding? She knew from Joanie exactly why Tommy was talking about seeing other people. But I guess being a born storyteller has its advantages. You learn to be very convincing.

"Come on, Terri. I'm sure you've been told about Tommy and me at Fritzie's." I heard the

18

bitterness in my own voice. "It must be nice to have such good friends."

She didn't lie. "I knew," she said, "but it didn't bother me too much. Tommy and I have been going together since seventh grade. I mean, *who* could possibly come between us? Besides, I always thought Joanie and Laura and Sandy might be exaggerating, making too much out of the times you went after their guys. I *defended* you more than once."

"Wonderful," I said, suddenly feeling frightened and very defensive. "It's so nice of you to stand up for me. So much easier than calling me once in a while, asking *me* what the story is. Easier to just go along with the rest and treat me like . . . *a leper*."

"No one trusts you anymore, Susan," she said calmly. "It's one thing to hack around and flirt with each other's guys when we're all together. We've always kind of done that. But it's another thing when you go behind our backs and move in."

"You all make me sick," I said. "Just because I'm nice to a guy, know how to talk to him, you think . . ."

"I *think* I don't trust you anymore either. I *think* you worked on Tommy, made him think you were just dying to go out with him. I *think* the girls are right."

I got up and grabbed up my tray.

"Think what you like, Terri. But I don't want any of your guys — not one of them. Not Gregg, or Larry, or Ronnie. Least of all, your precious

19

Tommy. Who needs them? I've got John. He beats everyone by a mile!"

I fought back the tears. Who did Terri think she was, accusing me like this. It wasn't fair. What had I really done?

Terri's voice wasn't angry or bitter or sarcastic, just sad. "I'd hold onto John if I were you, Susan. He's a nice guy."

"I intend to," I said, straightening my shoulders, lifting my chin. "And it won't be too hard. I'm the supposed expert, remember?"

But on the way to art class, I had to really work at keeping my shoulders straight, my chin up. I felt terrible — definitely not as sure and tough as I had made myself out to be with Terri. And why had I gotten so huffy with her, so defensive and nasty? Maybe she would have listened if I had just tried to explain. I had been honest when I said I didn't want Tommy or any of the other guys; it was just that . . .

Just what? How could I have explained? I didn't understand myself. Terri Lannigan was just like the others. If they wanted to gang up on me — *hate* me — let them. There was nothing I could do about it now. I only wished I could stop thinking about the tears I had seen glistening in Terri's gray eyes, and the sadness I heard in her voice. I certainly hadn't wanted to hurt Terri; I just . . .

"There are lots of good ideas here," Mrs. Petrie, the art teacher said, "but most of them have been done before. I'm looking for something new, something original, an idea that would

fire you all up, make you use your imaginations"
— she laughed — "not to mention your research
skills."

It was a relief to have something else to think
about. I paid close attention to what the teacher
was saying. Mrs. Petrie was talking about the
junior dance to be held on May first — May
Day — the biggest event of the school year.
Traditionally it was a costume thing, and
traditionally it is the art teacher (creative and
all that) who is the dance advisor. A couple of
weeks ago, she had asked us to submit ideas for
the theme of it. Whoever came up with the best
idea would be dance chairman. I submitted my
own idea without any big desire to work on the
dance, and I had forgotten all about it until this
moment. Now I could feel my curiosity rising.
Who would be the genius this year?

"Last year was just a little bit too simple," Mrs.
Petrie was saying.

She was right. Last year's dance had been
Greek-style — a toga party. Everyone just wore a
sheet and sandals, very easy. It hadn't cost anyone a penny or a thought.

"Now, this year, I think we do have one very
good, original idea," she said, "Something I think
would be lots of fun — and *work* — for everyone."

She paused and smiled almost slyly.

"Only one slight problem. . . ."

She had everyone's attention now and she
knew it.

"The one idea was submitted by two different
people. I'm quite sure it's a case of independent

21

thought. *Maybe* a coincidence, or as I sometimes believe, a case of being tuned in to the same source, or maybe to each other."

Someone in the back row groaned, and the rest of us had to laugh. Mrs. Petrie was constantly doing that, analyzing the smallest thing, philosophizing, never getting to the point. This time she took the hint.

"Okay, okay," she said, "All I'm really saying is that we have a dilemma on our hands. Because we can't have two top dogs, can we?"

"*Co*-chairmen," Tad Pollard said in a condescending voice. "Hasn't anyone ever heard of co-chairmen?"

"Sure," Mrs. Petrie said, "But what would you call them if they were not *men*?" Besides her mystical bent, the art teacher leaned toward feminism. Or as I suspected, she more than leaned but she wasn't *heavy* about it.

Tad Pollard looked truly disgusted. "You mean both of the winners are girls?"

Mrs. Petrie nodded, smiling.

"Chair*women*," Tammy White said triumphantly.

"Come *on*," Randy Hilsen said impatiently. "Who cares about titles. Who *won*? And what's this great idea?"

"You're absolutely right, Randy, the co-chair*persons* are . . ." Mrs. Petrie couldn't resist pausing one more time — a mystic, a feminist, an actress too. "Debbie Gilmore and Susan Bond."

My very first thought was: *who on earth is Debbie Gilmore*? It really isn't surprising that I didn't know everyone in every class, Appleby

High is a big school. Besides, when you stick so close with the same crowd since junior high days, it's understandable that lots of kids go unnoticed.

"Fine," Randy said, giving us his approval, "Now what's the theme?"

"It's a super idea, I think," Mrs. Petrie said. "In fact, it will be called SUPERBALL."

"Superbowl?" Lars Hansen asked hopefully. Lars is Appleby High's football star. "As in football?"

"No, Lars, as in Superman," the teacher said. "As in all the superheroes of comic book and cartoon and television fame. Wonder Woman, Batman and Robin . . ."

"Spider-Man, Captain America, Plastic Man," Tad added knowingly, and then looked puzzled, "How about the Six Million Dollar Man and The Incredible Hulk? Do they qualify?"

"Sure, they do," Mark Levy said firmly. "And that's exactly who I'm going to be, The Incredible Hulk."

Everyone laughed. Mark is the smallest, skinniest boy in the eleventh grade.

Now even Randy was interested. "Hey, we could make a real Batcave and. . . ."

Mrs. Petrie interrupted. "That will be up to the chairpersons, Debbie and Susan. Of course, I'm sure they'll be looking for good committee people, and they'll be receptive to all your ideas."

The teacher looked directly at me. "How about it, Susan? Are you open to ideas?"

I made myself smile and nod agreeably, but I was not sure yet if I liked this . . . this *honor*.

Especially since I didn't even know this Debbie person.

"How about you, Debbie?"

Mrs. Petrie had half-turned to the right and was looking at the fat girl in the seat nearest the window. I groaned inwardly. She was not my type at all — short; too heavy; thick, untidy eyebrows; do-nothing dark hair. I *had* noticed her once or twice before, I remembered. I had thought, at those times, that she wore the worst clothes possible for her particular figure (if you could call it that). Maybe it's because I'm so interested in clothes that I notice things like that.

Now I noticed how she ducked her head and lowered her eyes when Mrs. Petrie spoke to her. I did another groan-groan; obviously she was painfully shy as well as being painful to look at. Some Wonder Woman she'd make.

And then I was totally ashamed of myself. Always before, I thought my observations about someone else's looks or wardrobe stemmed from a kind of friendly concern — a natural desire to figure out how to make someone look better. Mom understood that; she felt the same way. I had almost decided to study retailing when I graduated. But now, I had to admit, I had been just plain mean. Debbie Gilmore was probably a very nice girl. I forced myself to smile at her, and she returned my smile, although hesitantly. I was right. She was very shy, very unsure of herself.

"Fine, then," Mrs. Petrie said, "See me after class, girls, and we'll go over your duties. After that, you can get together at your convenience. Just remember to keep me posted on your progress. Personally, I'm excited about this idea. I think it's going to be a great success."

She changed the subject then, asking us to work in charcoal, but *neatly*.

"I've seen more charcoal on the floor than I have on any of your papers," she said, adding. "Of course, it's not me who's complaining. Mr. Mayo is screaming again."

Mr. Mayo, one of the custodians, was well-known to us. We often saw him lurking around the artroom door during class. He always wore an expression of intense displeasure when he saw we were painting in oils or doing papier mâché. You could read his mind: *damn kids messing up my room again*. Mr. Mayo, whatever he was, was certainly not an art lover.

In a way, I was. I really liked Mrs. Petrie's class and Mrs. Petrie herself. And, I thought, it would be kind of fun to work on the dance, the decorations, my costume. If only I had someone good to work on it with. But I caught myself just in time. Who was I to criticize Debbie? It had been a long time since I had won any popularity contests.

CHAPTER THREE

No wonder Debbie Gilmore is fat; her mother is always putting food in front of her. When I've been there, she tries to do it to me too.

She fixes a big platter of sandwiches — sandwiches crammed with lunch meat, cheese, tomatoes, globs of mayonnaise. She sets out dishes of pickles, olives, cole slaw, potato salad, and after that, chocolate cake.

Mrs. Gilmore stands nearby, smiling at us, asking anxiously, "How's everything, girls — okay?"

She calls it, "Just a little something to tide you over until suppertime."

Steve, Debbie's brother, gets a tray in his room so he can do his homework and read his comic books undisturbed. Steve is eleven, very bright, and fat.

I'm sure when Debbie's mother looks at me, she is seeing all the starving people in the world. Not that I'm skinny, no one has ever said that. But I am tall and my weight is pretty evenly distributed. Slim, I guess you'd say. Still, Mrs. Gilmore worries about me and insists, "You need a little more meat on your bones, Susan."

She says it kindly, and she is always nice to me, but it is obvious that she really does worry about health a lot. The kitchen counter is lined with big bottles of vitamins, from A to E, and the cabinet in their bathroom could be a branch of Appleby Pharmacy.

That explains Debbie's wardrobe too. Mrs. Gilmore picks out all the clothing for her family, and since "wool is warm" and "big is better," everything Debbie owns is bulky, tweedy, heavy, *wrong*.

Poor Debbie. She really is quite nice, and I'm beginning to enjoy being with her, but she has a hard time of it. Trying to please her mother, being "a good kid," is ruining her. Good, according to Mrs. Gilmore's standards, means fat. Even *Mr.* Gilmore is overweight.

But Mrs. Gilmore is *thin*. I mean trim, slim, thin, a perfect size seven. She picks at her food like Mrs. Pulaski's Katya.

If I thought at first I wouldn't have anything in common with Debbie, if I thought I was superior in some way, I was wrong. Actually, we are very much alike in many ways, not even mentioning the fact that we don't count for anything socially; Debbie, not ever; me not anymore. But if it sounds as if it's misery loves company, it isn't. We discovered that we are both *Little Rascal* addicts. The fact that we've watched the same movies over and over again doesn't spoil our pleasure one bit. Debbie and I laugh as if we were seeing Spanky and Alfalfa and Buckwheat for the first time. We laugh too about things that we notice other people take very seriously, such as the weather, or sports scores, or politicians. All highly unpredictable, Debbie says, so why bother? Also, I've found Debbie is a fantastic mimic. Debbie really cracks me up.

Debbie *is* shy, but around me, not so much anymore. Still, I've noticed, most of her humor consists of jokes about herself, putting herself down. A sense of humor about your own faults is fine, I guess, as long as you don't overdo it. Debbie overdoes it, and finally, I told her so.

"You're too hard on yourself," I said. "Besides, when you say you're clumsy, and completely uncoordinated, people will be watching for that. It will make you even more self-conscious and you *will* be clumsy."

"But it's true, Susan," she said. "When I enter a room, the legs of the table take two steps back to avoid me."

"See?" I said. "You're doing it again. And now what am I supposed to say, 'Yeah, Debbie, you really are a klutz'? Because I don't think it's true. I've watched the way you move. You're really quite graceful."

Debbie made a disgusted face.

"Oh, sure. Haven't you heard? All fat people are light on their feet, regular twinkle-toes. It's a cliché."

It was the first time she had ever brought up the subject of weight. I knew it bothered her to be so heavy; I had seen the expression in her eyes when she caught a glimpse of herself in a full-length mirror or a store window. When I took her to meet Mrs. Pulaski for the first time, Debbie saw the freshly baked *chrusciki* and looked away quickly, as if the pastry were a dreaded enemy. During our visit, Mrs. Pulaski mentioned Mrs. Pratt two doors down and the fact that she was going to Weight Watchers.

"Good thing," Mrs. Pulaski said. "She lose her husband if she don't watch out."

I know Mrs. Pulaski wouldn't have said that if she thought it would hurt my friend's feelings. It was just neighborhood news. But I noticed then how miserable Debbie looked. So now, since she brought it up, I plunged in.

"Listen, Debbie, you wouldn't be . . . you wouldn't have a weight problem if you just didn't eat all that stuff in between meals. Cut out the snacking and I bet you'd start losing, fast."

Her eyes lit up briefly and then clouded again.

"It's just that I hate to hurt Mom's feelings. She goes to all that trouble for us every day."

"Hey, Debbie," I said firmly. "I don't want to say anything against your mother but *she* is your problem. Start saying no to her. Of course, in a nice way. Maybe if she sees you don't keel over and die from lack of food, she'll let up a little — help you diet. You know what I mean?"

"Yes, I do. But Mom is so nervous. And do you know, Susan? I think it's Mom's way of show- ing affection, loving us, Dad and Steve and me. What am I supposed to say to that? No thanks? It would probably *kill* her."

"No, it won't," I said.

I dropped the subject *that* day, but after that, I began to give her pep talks, trying to encourage her to stop eating so much.

"You have such a pretty face, Debbie," I said one day. "If only . . ."

She snorted rudely: "*Come* on, Susan, stop giving me all these clichés. I *don't* have a pretty face. It's too round and soft and pasty; my face is about as exciting as tapioca pudding."

"Stop doing that to yourself," I said fiercely. "And besides, if you must know, tapioca is one of my favorites. I *love* tapioca! And anyway," I continued, "you can't judge. You have no idea what you'd look like with your bones showing in your face — *cheekbones* — and the right makeup, a new hairstyle."

I thought she would change the subject as she usually did, back to our dance plans or something unthreatening, but this time, she looked interested.

"Cheekbones? Do you really think I have cheekbones?"

I laughed. "Of course you do, silly. *Everyone* has cheekbones."

I let it drop because I didn't want to push too hard. Debbie had to want it for herself. Meanwhile, I decided, I'll keep my ideas to myself . . . my ideas for The Great Gilmore Makeover. I was ready the moment she was.

Planning the SUPERBALL was more like play than work. We sat and tossed ideas around like tennis balls and neither of us seemed to miss a serve. I was tempted to tell Mrs. Petrie that she had been right on target. Debbie and I *were* in tune with each other. We hand-picked a committee and after that, we all met in the artroom every Monday and Wednesday after school. The dance wasn't until May, but there was lots to do before then: printing tickets, hiring a band, making decorations.

Randy Hilsen was determined to design and construct an elaborate Batcave. He offered to buy Debbie and me a Coke at Fritzie's so we could listen to his plans without interruption. Debbie was excited. Can you believe it? Debbie has never been to Fritzie's in her life.

I hadn't been there since that time with Terri's boyfriend Tommy — he *did* call me and I *did* turn him down — but wouldn't you know, when Randy, Debbie, and I walked in, the first faces I saw were Joanie's, Sandy's, and Laura's. Unfortunately, the only empty booth was the one directly next to them. Don't worry about it, I told myself — you're with good friends. How could my old — friends — hurt me? They didn't matter to me anymore, did they? I knew one thing for sure, *I* didn't matter to them.

But I underestimated Joanie Sangerville. She's not really a cruel person, but she's a busybody, if you know what I mean, and for as long as I've known her, she has had mouth trouble. Sometimes, it's a matter of blurting out something stupid because she hasn't thought about it first. Other times it's an attempt to get a laugh. When I was friends with her, it used to be kind of funny; you never knew what Joanie would come out with.

Now, behind me, I heard whispering, and I caught, "No . . . you *can't. Joanie, no!*"

But apparently Joanie was determined to do

her thing. She stood up and there she was suddenly at our table.

"Hi," she said brightly, *too* brightly. "Are you all working on the dance?"

"Yes, we are," Randy said, not hiding his impatience. "We were just *about* to."

She didn't get the message.

"We all love the idea, of course, but we're having a problem — what to wear? What did you decide on?"

She was looking at Randy. He rolled his eyes.

"If I knew, I wouldn't tell you," he said. "Do you think I want to spoil my grand entrance?"

Joanie was undaunted. "How about you?" she said, gesturing at Debbie. *You*, I thought. That was nice. She didn't even know Debbie's name, and couldn't be bothered asking. But Debbie looked pleased as well as flustered at the unaccustomed attention.

"I really don't know yet," she said politely.

"And you, Susan? Who will you be?"

Joanie's voice was friendly enough, but it was easy enough for me to detect the false note. I knew Joanie well enough to know she had something up her sleeve.

I shrugged, trying to appear nonchalant.

"Haven't really thought about it yet," I said. "The dance isn't until May so we all have plenty of time."

I waited for her to make her point. There *had* to be a point. Joanie wasn't being all cutsie and friendly for nothing.

"Well, if you need some ideas . . ." she said and then stopped.

Her faced reddened, and I could see she was trying very hard not to laugh. I could hear muffled laughter from behind me.

"Oh, well, never mind," she said, turning and disappearing back in her booth.

Randy, Debbie, and I exchanged looks as if to say, "What's her problem," when I heard, very distinctly, from behind, the words: ". . . go as . . . *Superflirt*."

So that was what Joanie had planned to say — a kind suggestion for me, for my costume. Superflirt, huh? Very funny, I thought, very cute. A typical Joanie idea. I could almost feel sorry for her. Always, as long as I had known her, she played the clown, the daredevil, the outrageous one. I remembered how we used to get her to say and do things we were afraid to do. So maybe it wasn't Joanie's idea, most likely it had been a group effort.

Now, with time to think about a reply, I almost wished she had dared to say it. "Superflirt? Sure, Joanie, maybe I will." And then I would have given her the definition of super: "beyond ordinary human ability, power, experience."

And then I could have suggested the perfect costume for her, for all of them: Catwoman.

I noticed Debbie looking at me, and there was sympathy in her eyes. She raised her eyebrows, and grimaced, as if to say: nuts to them. Bless her. At that moment, I knew Debbie was a real friend.

We made Randy very happy by ooohing and ahhhing over his Batcave drawings. He was so happy he wanted to treat us to a cheeseburger, but I said no, and so did Debbie. We had to get home, plus I had had all I could take of the whisperings and gigglings in the next booth.

Debbie and I walked toward home; we lived only three blocks apart. She was quiet and so was I.

"May I ask you a personal question, Susan?" she asked finally.

"Sure," I said. "Ask."

"How come you don't go around with those girls anymore? I used to see you all the time, together."

I was startled, and then I felt guilty. Debbie had been aware of me for a long time apparently, and I hadn't known she was alive!

"They hate me because they think I tried to steal their boyfriends away," I said truthfully, then added: "As if I'd want to."

I didn't look at her.

"Maybe you should worry about being friends with me," I said seriously. "Who knows? Maybe I'll steal your guy away."

Debbie laughed. "I don't have anything to worry about, Susan, and you know it. I don't have a boyfriend to my name."

Her smile faded. "And you also know that my working on the SUPERBALL is a laugh and a half. I won't even get to go to the thing. Who's going to ask me?"

"Of course you . . ." I stopped in mid-sentence and stared at her.

She was right! Who *would* ask her to the dance? Certainly, since I had known her, I had never seen a boy give her a second glance. But it was terrible, all wrong. Debbie was working so hard and contributing so much toward making the dance the best ever. I stopped walking suddenly and put my hand on her arm.

"Listen, Debbie! You *are* going to the dance. But you are going to have to cooperate." I glared at her. "*Starting today, you are not going to eat between meals.* During the next month or maybe six weeks, you are going to lose at least ten pounds. You *are* going to have cheekbones!"

I eyed her uneven, lank dark hair. "And we're going to think of something great to do to your hair."

She opened her mouth.

"*Shut up,*" I said in a mock fierce voice. "You are in my power now. You are going to do exactly what I say. You, Debbie Gilmore, are going to discover your best self!"

"But Susan," she said weakly, "My mom. . . ."

"It probably will be difficult at first," I said, "so you might have to be sneaky about it. *Pretend* to eat. But, Debbie, spit it out, stuff it in your pocket, anything, *just don't swallow.* Also, go easy on bread, butter, potatoes, desserts — small portions of *everything.*"

Her eyes were wide and her mouth opened again as if to protest.

"Quiet!" I commanded. "Exercise. We will walk a mile a day for the first week, then work up to two and then three."

"Susan!" Debbie was laughing now. At that moment I knew I had her. I caught the look of hope and delight in her eyes.

I patted her on the shoulder. "Just do everything I tell you and you'll go to the dance — with someone really nice." I smiled at her and put my hand over my heart. "I *promise*."

"It's a nice thought," she began doubtfully.

"It is *not* a thought," I said firmly. "I said *promise*. You're going to be so gorgeous, I'll probably hate you."

She shook her head. "I'll never be *gorgeous*," she said, "No matter how much weight I lose. I'm plain, naturally plain, tapioca-face, remember?"

"And *you* remember, I love tapioca. But you're not naturally plain and I'm going to prove it to you, Debbie."

"Oh, Susan," she said ever so softly, "I'm so glad you're my friend."

I gave her my wickedest grin. "You are now," I said. "But just wait. During the next six weeks there will be lots of times when you'll wish you never met me. I plan to be very demanding — a regular *slavedriver*."

Her smile said "thank you."

I didn't say it out loud, but inwardly I was thanking her too.

Thank you, Debbie Gilmore, for giving my life a new purpose — something to do every day and on weekends. Thank you because now I have someone to talk to, laugh with. And she thought I was doing something for *her*. If she *only* knew!

CHAPTER FOUR

By the end of the first week, Debbie had lost four pounds. She was thrilled; her mother was not. She acted out the scene for me.

"Are you sure you're feeling all right, Debbie?" Mrs. Gilmore had said. "I don't know. You don't look *right* to me."

Debbie had her mother down pat: the anxious voice, the worried look in her eye, the hovering. I had to laugh. Luckily Debbie has developed a sense of humor about her mother. She laughed too.

"And she keeps wanting to make special stuff for me — eggnogs, rice dumplings, pudding — all nice, warm, fluffy stuff. Sometimes lately I've been wondering if she knows I'm sixteen years old?"

She was beginning to see the situation more clearly now. Good. It would make my job easier.

I teased her. "You really have a thing against pudding, don't you, Debbie?"

She stuck out her tongue at me, and suddenly brought her face up close to mine.

"Do you see any signs of cheekbones yet?" she asked, sucking in her cheeks like mad.

I studied her face carefully. "Possibly — a *hint*. But you have a ways to go, maybe next week."

"Oh," she said, disappointed. "I thought the reason Mom was panicking was because she saw bones. I think Mom *hates* bones."

I didn't pursue the subject. I was just happy that Debbie was learning to resist her mother. On the other hand, I didn't want to be the cause of bad feelings between them. In all other ways, I like Mrs. Gilmore. She's a nice person and a good mother.

The same with my mother. I don't think she is always aware of what she is doing either. She seems to hide from problems, from life. If, once in a while, her temper flares and she stands up for herself and me, most of the time she takes the easy way out, saying nothing, changing the subject, smoothing things over. As soon as Daddy leaves for work, she gathers up Puddy-Cat, a book, a cup of coffee, goes into her bedroom, and shuts the door. She "hides out" from her friends, the world, *me*.

Sometimes, I want to shake her, yell at her. "What's the matter with you? Where's your old spirit?" I want to ask, "What is the matter with Daddy?"

But I've never asked, and now, it's not quite as important to me. I'm not around the house as much as before. Just as well — Daddy seems to be getting worse. He's been a grouch for so long, he's getting lines in his forehead and around his mouth. He looks older. He rarely pays any attention to me; he always seems to have something more important on his mind.

I guess I've picked up some of Mom's tricks because now I avoid it all. What can I do about the situation at home? Nothing, as far as I can see.

Tonight when John came to pick me up, he asked if my parents had gone out.

"No," I said. "Daddy's sleeping, and Mom's in the spare room reading.

"Oh," he said, "I thought . . . I mean, the house is so quiet."

I nodded. The house was always quiet. It had a certain heavy stillness to it, which I thought was different from quiet — a gloomy atmosphere that made me uncomfortable. John too, I guess. He certainly could remember a time, not so long ago, when Mom and Daddy were very much in evidence, talking, laughing, teasing John, fussing over me, asking where we were going, what time we'd be getting home. No wonder I had used that line about being an orphan; I *felt* like one sometimes.

"What would you rather do, Susan, a party or a movie?"

He put his head back, and looked at me from under his eyelashes the way I love him to do. John is so good-looking, I think, but not in the usual, handsome way. He has dark, curly hair (he thinks it is *too* curly) and the kind of ruddy, healthy complexion you get from spending a lot of time outdoors. He has a nose I like, and his eyes are what I call Hershey Bar brown. And they melt too, at least they seem to when he's feeling especially romantic.

39

He was watching me closely, and I could tell he was trying to figure out what kind of mood I was in.

"Where's the party?" I asked. I tried hard to keep the resentment out of my voice, but it hurt not knowing, not being part of it anymore. It was humiliating having to depend on John to know what was going on with kids my own age.

"Ronnie's house," he said. "He helped his father convert their garage into a family room. He helped him with the understanding that, when it was finished, he'd get to throw a big party. You know Ronnie — big wheeler-dealer." He laughed. "Should be fun though, don't you think?"

I didn't answer that. "Who's going to be there?" I asked instead.

Dopey question. Who else? All my friends who were not my friends anymore. John certainly knew the situation, but in his mind, they were all wrong, probably just jealous. Any rumors he heard, he brushed off with, "They're nuts. You're *my* girl!"

When we did go to parties, John always made up for the coolness toward me with an extra amount of affection and attentiveness. He made sure I never got stuck sitting in a corner by myself; we either danced together, or sat quietly, holding hands and talking or listening to the music.

Not that we were both outcasts — far from it. Plenty of people paid attention to John. Everyone liked him; there is nothing about John not to like. He is easygoing, quick to laugh, a good sport.

But for me a party is more like a punishment.

40

It just isn't any fun to be around people who you know don't like you. Still, John looked eager and I knew he was looking forward to seeing his friends, a reward after working hard all week.

"Okay, to the party then," I said.

It wouldn't kill me and I wanted to please him. John is wonderful.

I went to the hall closet to get my coat and I hunted for what seemed like a long time for my scarf and gloves. I had put them on the shelf in the closet; I was sure of it.

"I can't find my scarf," I wailed, "or my gloves."

John was suddenly right beside me, very close, and then his arms were around me.

"Don't cry," he whispered, "I'll keep you warm."

He kissed me, and every trace of irritability vanished.

My arms were around his neck now and I held tight.

"Oh, John," I whispered back, "You're so good to me. Why are you so good to me?"

He pulled his head back and did his eyelash thing to me.

"Why shouldn't I be good to you, Susan Bee? I *love* you."

John started that Susan Bee thing a long time ago. When I first starting learning about Women's Liberation, I was amazed that women had been fighting for equal rights such a long time ago. One of the women especially fascinated me — Susan B. Anthony. I was much slower than John and Mom to see it. They said if I married John, that is exactly what my name would be, if I just used the initial B for Bond. So now, in moments of fun or affection, both Mom and John called me Susan Bee.

John can say "I love you" so easily, so sincerely, there is no doubt in my mind that he does. And that *is* John, direct, honest, kind. And of course, because he is so honest, he thinks everyone else is too. I don't think he ever has a bad thought about anyone. To him, everyone is "a great guy" or "a great girl."

I suppose that's why John still loves me, *can* love me, no matter what anyone says about me. He only sees my good points, only what he wants to see. I think I would feel better if he saw my flaws too, and *then* loved me anyway.

He held me for a few more minutes until we both heard a door close upstairs. Probably Daddy waking up; in an hour or so he would have to start getting ready for work.

"Come on, John," I said. "Let's go now."

Suddenly I couldn't wait to get away from the oppressive stillness of my house. I wanted to be outside, moving, breathing fresh air.

"It really is a great night," John said, as we got into his old but well-kept Chevy. "Look at those stars."

We both peered through the windshield for a moment, stargazing, and then he put the key in the ignition and started the car. As we pulled away from the curb, I saw him glance back toward my house.

"Boy, you live on a quiet street," he said. "It's deserted."

"Well, John," I said, "We'll have to liven it up."

John said, clucking at me, "Did anyone ever tell you you're a funny girl?"

Immediately he began to sing a made-up tune with made-up words.

I know a fun-ny girl her name is Susan Bee . . .
I love that funny girl and I think . . .
oh, I thinkkk . . .
she loves meeee . . .

I moved over close and kissed his cheek.

"Yesss . . . she loves you. . . ." I sang back to him.

That's what I mean about John — he sees the bright side, the happy side. He doesn't ever seem to see the flip side of things: gloom, sadness, worry. Lucky John, and because of him, lucky me too, I thought. He won't allow me to be down in the dumps tonight.

"I'll have to fill the gas tank before we go," he said. "Right now we're riding on empty. Good thing Dad paid me tonight."

He said it very cheerfully. Even if some people don't complain about anything else, they *do* complain about the price of gas.

We pulled into the Mobil station, a brightly lit oasis on the line between Appleby and East Springwood. Three young guys in white coveralls were lounging around in the office. We could see them there drinking soda, laughing.

"Hey, there's Frankie Thomas," John said happily. "I didn't know he worked here. Do you mind if I leave you for a sec . . . say hello?"

"Sure, go ahead," I said, taking my comb out

43

of my pocket and pulling down the sun visor where John had mounted a good-sized mirror just for me.

John went to see his friend and I concentrated on my hair. For a change it was doing just what I wanted it to do. But I'm weird, I guess, because that's when I fool with it the most, try to get it to do other things, and end up ruining it. Big deal, I thought as I combed. It's only hair.

I didn't notice him at first, I was so busy trying to make my hair flip forward. But when I put the mirror up, he was there in my view suddenly, wiping the windshield, staring at me, a small smile hovering around his mouth.

"Hi!" I said automatically, although I knew he probably couldn't hear me with the car windows closed. It didn't matter; he understood. He said hi back, and gave me a real smile, all the while rubbing the windshield.

I stole a quick glance toward the office. John had his back toward me, and I could see his hands moving, describing something.

This guy was really cute — too short for me, maybe, but . . .

Suddenly I was *doing* it. It's hard to explain exactly what I do at times like this, and it's not as if I *plan* it or anything. I just feel myself brightening inside; I gather my forces sort of, and then flash it all outward toward . . . *whoever*. When it happens, I know my eyes are sparkling, my color is higher, and my face is alive. At that moment I do feel brighter, prettier, and there is a little voice somewhere inside me that is asking: *Am I pretty? Tell me, tell me.*

I guess that's what flirting is — *my* flirting anyway. Except, I never ask that question. Never. It wouldn't be flirting then, would it? It would be begging.

Besides, why would I even have to ask if I'm pretty or nice of anyone, especially some strange boy who is definitely way too short for me?

But I could tell he thought so. He was motioning for me to roll down the window. I rolled the window down halfway.

"What?" I asked, making my eyes very wide.

"You live around here?" Shortie asked.

"Sure," I said. "Do you?"

"Now," he said. "New York before — Brooklyn."

"Brooklyn? Aren't you supposed to talk funny?" I tilted my head when I looked at him.

He grinned. "Am I? Who told you that?"

Now he had his face very close to the open window, very close. Out of the corner of my eye, I saw John coming out of the office. When he saw Shortie talking to me he paused for a second, but he didn't look annoyed.

"Hey, fella," he said as he approached his car. "Fill my tank, not my girl's ear." He said it good-naturedly and we laughed.

Shortie gave John a salute. "Yessir, right away, sir."

We all laughed again, friends. But when John was fishing in his pocket for money, and his eyes were down, Shortie winked at me. He moved his mouth. "Beau-ti-ful," he said silently.

As we drove away from the station, John put a hand over my hand and squeezed it tight.

45

"Better stay real close to me tonight, Susan Bee. I know you can't help it, but every guy walking seems to want to take you away from me. Maybe I should get you a great big guard dog for protection when I'm not around."

I laughed. "Don't worry, John. You don't have to worry. I can take care of myself." I squeezed his hand for reasurance, for him or for myself, I wasn't quite sure. "Anyway," I said, "I don't want every guy walking. I love *you*."

"That's my girl," he said happily.

And I am your girl, John, I thought. I really am. The other stuff, the flirting stuff, didn't mean anything. Not anything at all.

CHAPTER FIVE

Either Ronnie and his father had made the new family room too small, or he had invited too many kids to his party: the room was packed to overflowing with bodies.

John and I managed to find a space for ourselves, but for the first few minutes, we just stood there, not speaking, trying to absorb the scene and the music, make some sense of it.

I looked up at John. He was grinning, and there was an expression of joy on his face. It was obvious that he really liked being at this party, with his friends, even if it meant being a sardine all evening.

"Hey, John, what's up?"

It was Ronnie, playing host in the only way possible; yelling across the crowded room, pointing toward the refreshment table.

The bodies next to us turned to see who Ronnie was yelling at, and suddenly, we were part of a group.

"John, when did you arrive? Didn't see you come in. Matter of fact. . . ."

The rest of Gregg Brooks' sentence was

drowned out by a burst of loud laughter. He grinned and shrugged and tried again.

"How's the heavy Chevy running, John? And when are you going to sell it to me?"

John laughed but he shook his head emphatically. "*Never!*" he said. "I know what I've got; I got lucky when I bought that car."

"Yeah, you sure did," Gregg said ruefully. "*I* should be so lucky." He turned toward the two boys standing with him. "Have you guys ever seen John's set of wheels?"

Immediately all four boys began talking cars with the easy enthusiasm that subject seems to inspire in them. But I didn't feel left out; just the opposite, I was beginning to enjoy myself. The two boys with Gregg were strangers to me, and they appeared to be a little older than the rest of the crowd. I found out I was right about that, when I heard them say they were home on leave from the Navy. They had graduated the year before. Both were quite good-looking, but better than that, I could tell they thought I was too. Especially the tall one with the big blue eyes. He couldn't seem to stop looking at me, even while he held up his end of the car conversation.

Naturally, I looked back. No harm in that. I was sure that John was happy to have me standing there beside him, but it was a very pleasant feeling to know that I was interesting to someone else too. And I didn't have to say a word — all it took was an occasional faint smile, a glance at him now and then. It really was a very nice situation — me, surrounded by four great-looking guys. So what if not one girl had said "hi" to me?

It got better. Suddenly, Ronnie was squeezing in beside John, and following him were two other guys we knew. I felt like a queen. Ronnie smiled at me and shook his head.

"Poor Susan, hasn't anyone ever told you you can't have all the fun? There are six or seven girls sitting all alone over there, and here you are, hogging all the guys."

He said it teasingly. He wasn't being sarcastic. I smiled at him, a big wide smile, and tossed my head.

"Not *poor* Susan, Ronnie, *lucky* Susan," I said. "This is a *great* party. In fact, this is the *best* party you ever had."

I linked my arm through his and leaned close to him. "Have another one next week, okay?"

Everyone in our group laughed. "She's got the right idea, Ronnie," John said. "Except maybe you should go back to work on this room, make it bigger. What did you do? Invite the world?"

"I think he did," I said gaily. "But so what? I think it's great. It's fun to meet new people."

I felt, rather than saw, Blue-Eyes look at me, and I knew *he* knew I had meant that last remark for him. I waited for a while before I allowed myself to smile at him, but when I did, his answering smile was a warm one, meant just for me. I was sure no one else had noticed.

But John had noticed that I was standing there empty-handed.

"Oh, wow — I'm sorry, Susan. You must be thirsty. Stay put and I'll get you a Coke or something."

49

"How can I do anything else?" I said teasingly. "If I moved I might get crushed."

"Protect her, will you?" John said, as he began his hard journey to the refreshment table. He hadn't meant that for anyone in particular but Blue-Eyes took it as a personal order. He shifted position so that he was standing beside me.

"Can't let *you* get crushed," he said, smiling down at me. "That would be a real shame, Susan."

He really was moving in, in every sense of the word. He probably didn't know that John and I . . .

"Do you like to dance?" he asked. "If it wasn't so crowded, I would love to dance with you. I could show you this new dance I learned."

"I *do* love to dance," I said. "But it's impossible." I laughed. "Unless we got up on the table or something."

He laughed with me. "Now *that*'s an idea. Let's do it."

Suddenly he had me by the hand and he was moving into the crowd, making a path for me.

"We'll clear off that big table," he said over his shoulder.

"We'll give this crew an exhibition."

I pulled my hand away, and stopped short. I wanted to — or at least part of me did. It would be fun, daring, *exciting*.

"I can't," I said. "Not here."

He looked at me, and his eyes lit up. "Want to go somewhere else? We can leave."

I was nervous, but I smiled at Blue-Eyes. He was too fast for me, and I could see John coming toward us now. What was he going to think?

"Can't," I said hastily, still smiling at him. "My boyfriend. . . ."

Blue-Eyes looked at me and then at John. His eyes, for the first time, seemed cool and indifferent.

"Could have fooled me," he muttered, as he moved back into position beside Gregg. In a little while, they all drifted away, leaving John and me alone again.

John seemed quiet suddenly, maybe even distant. It was less crowded now, and even the music had been turned down enough so we could hear ourselves talk. Except we weren't talking; I realized John hadn't said a word since he came back with the Cokes.

Then he asked, "What was that all about, Susan? Where were you going with that guy?"

I was shocked at the anger in his voice, but I made my eyes wide and innocent when I looked at him.

"Why, John, I'm surprised at you. You actually sound worried. He had some wild idea about showing everyone how to do this new dance that he learned. He decided I was going to help him demonstrate. Can you imagine that crazy guy, John? He wanted to dance on the *table*! I said 'no way.' I can just picture that — Ronnie's mother walking in and seeing me up on her table. Thank heavens you came back and saved me."

His face relaxed, but he didn't smile.

"I'm glad you didn't," he said solemnly.

I leaned against him, and rested my head against his shoulder.

"You don't have to worry, John," I whispered. "I told you that."

"I know," he said. "I remember."

That was the end of any more serious moments, because the door opened, and a new batch of kids filled up the room again, and John was immediately surrounded by admirers.

"Good to see you, Anthony. Where have you been hiding?"

"In the ditch I've been digging all week," John said, chuckling. "Tell these lazy guys how hard I work, Susan, while *they're* having a good time."

He sounded happy. With his friends, the party, and with me too. Everything was all right. I didn't have a thing to worry about.

CHAPTER SIX

Mrs. Gilmore was very upset; she tried to enlist her husband's help in getting Debbie to eat.

"Look at her, Phillip, something is wrong. She won't touch her food, and if she does she just *picks*. It's not right, it's not *healthy*. She's a growing girl."

Debbie recreated the scene, word for word, complete with worried voice and frown.

"And then guess what Dad said, Susan? He looked Mom straight in the eye and said, 'Debbie looks great — leave her alone.' "

She does look great; there is a new glow about her, a sheen to her skin. And she is definitely thinner, another few pounds this week.

Debbie sighed happily. "I can tell Dad is proud of me too. He just has that look in his eye that means 'Good for you,' and he smiles at me a lot more."

"That's terrific, Deb," I said and meant it. Still, I couldn't help feeling a little wistful. How long had it been since Daddy smiled at me?

"You know, Susan? I think my losing weight is giving Dad courage. Steve too. Mom made a chocolate layer cake and a lemon meringue pie on Tuesday and now it's Friday. No one has *touched* them. She'll have to throw them away." She paused. "Unless she decides to eat them herself."

"Debbie, remember how uncomplicated everything used to be? When I was real little, life seemed so simple. The stove was hot and the freezer was cold. Good was good and bad was bad; the truth was the truth and the lie was . . . well, you know what I mean. Now, it's as if some crazy, lazy spider made a huge web, and instead of making it perfect, as spiders are *supposed* to do, it left all kinds of loose ends dangling, parts tangled, or unfinished, and some of it just completely *wrong*." I tried to laugh. "That's it, Deb. Anything that's wrong with us, with our lives, we can blame on that incompetent spider."

"I do know what you mean," Debbie said. "And I guess it's easier, *safer*, not to analyze too much. Trouble with us, Susan, is that we think too much." She stopped walking. "Aren't we going to your house? I thought we were going to your house."

"You've got your money with you, don't you, Deb?" I asked.

"You told me to bring it but not to ask questions. I have twenty-two dollars — the last of my birthday money."

"Good girl," I said breezily, "You're going to need it."

I took her arm and steered her firmly toward the shopping district, specifically Appleby Pharmacy. In the past five years, the pharmacy has expanded a lot, growing from a dinky little hole-in-the-wall where you brought prescriptions to be filled to a very large store where you can find almost everything you need in the way of books, school supplies, gifts, leather goods, not to mention health and beauty aids. But today was the day *to* mention beauty aids. That's the reason I told Debbie to bring her money with her. It was time to start on the second phase of The Great Gilmore Makeover.

Debbie was overwhelmed by the array of cosmetics and hair products; it was a world she didn't know. Sometimes, not often, she wore lipstick, but that was all.

She needed everything so I asked Ellen Hendrix to wait on us. Ellen is a friend of Mom's, and she knows the products backward and forward. She is always helpful but she never pushes you to buy stuff you really don't need; in my opinion, the best kind of salesperson.

Anyway, I bought, or rather, *Debbie* bought: a home permanent, the gentle kind, guaranteed not to produce frizzies; a good conditioner, to keep Debbie's hair in shape, although her switch to a protein-rich diet had improved her hair a lot already; liquid makeup, the sheer kind, to even out her skin tones; blusher, the cream kind; a soft, heathery gray eye crayon; mascara; an eyelash curler; eyebrow tweezers; and a lipstick. I selected a clear, clean-looking coral. Nothing muddy, nothing too bright or greasy-looking.

I had a definite idea of how Debbie's face should look. I loved this; it was exciting.

Debbie was very impressed.

"How do you know all this, Susan? You sound like an expert."

Ellen Hendrix laughed. "I was thinking the same thing. Next thing you know, she'll be after my job."

She leaned over the counter and whispered in Debbie's ear. Her whisper was loud; I was meant to hear it.

"The truth is, everything Susan knows she learned at my knee. Notice how she doesn't give me any credit?"

I laughed and pretended to look very sheepish.

"She's right, Deb, I've haunted this place for years now. And Ellen gives me lots of good tips."

It came to nineteen fifty plus tax. Debbie was broke but I knew her groan was just for show; she was wildly excited. We had let Ellen in on the Makeover plans. Now she smiled at Debbie.

"Come back, will you? Show me how you look."

Debbie smiled and nodded. She really was looking good these days, even without any make-up. She was still wearing her bulky clothes, but it was quite obvious now that she wasn't bulky underneath. Eight and a half pounds had made an amazing difference. I figured another couple of pounds would do it, but now Debbie was the ambitious one. "More," she said.

Debbie thought we were going to my house, so she kept on walking even when I stopped in front of the Pulaski's house.

"What's the matter?" she said. "Why did you stop?"

"My father is sleeping and we're going to have to make some noise — water running and stuff. I asked Mrs. Pulaski if we could do your hair at her house. Naturally, she said yes. I think she was very happy too. She's alone so much."

"Will Mr. Pulaski be there?" Debbie asked. She knew how I felt about him.

"Uh unh, he's downtown as usual. Didn't you see him when we came out of the pharmacy? Sitting on the bench in the Square?"

"No, I didn't," Debbie said. "I guess I was too excited about the makeup and the permanent."

"Well, calm down," I said, as we walked up the porch steps. "You're not Wonder Woman yet."

I rang the doorbell. Debbie looked dreamy. "It's like that, isn't it?" she said. "All the super-heroes, male and female, have two identities. First, they are plain, dull, ordinary, then into a phonebooth, or behind a tree and wham! bang! They're special, gorgeous, powerful."

"Should we tell Mrs. Pulaski that her home is really a phonebooth? Maybe I better not, she might worry."

"Yes," she said. "The shock might be too much." Then she looked at me. "You're right, Susan, I better calm down. Besides, I don't believe in miracles. I mean, what can you really do with a tapioca face?"

I patted her face gently. "I've never seen tapioca with cheekbones."

"*Really? Really*, Susan?" She was excited again. She touched her own face, tracing the bones with her fingers. "I think . . . yes . . . I can *feel* them!

I could have saved Debbie twenty-two dollars if I could have bottled the ingredient that was coloring her face now, making it shine, making her eyes light up. Unfortunately, there is no way to bottle *hope.*

Mrs. Pulaski took one look at Debbie, understood immediately that she was on a diet, and went immediately to the kitchen to make tea. Clear, unsweetened tea with lemon for Debbie, mine with sugar and lots of milk the way I liked it. Mrs. Pulaski also put her day's baking away in the breadbox. I had a sudden thought: why not send Mrs. Gilmore over to Mrs. Pulaski for a few lessons. But of course, I didn't say it.

I can disapprove and even, sometimes, dislike Mom and Dad, and even *say* it to someone. But just let anyone else say a word against them, and I'm ready to defend them to the death. I guess most families are like that, loyal, no matter what.

Mrs. Pulaski suggested we use the guest bedroom because it has a nice, big bathroom of its own.

"I promise I will not bother you. I know girls have things to talk about."

She looked so wistful.

"Why do you think you'd be bothering us, Mrs. Pulaski? We came over here so you could help us. We're going to need your advice."

I saw the happiness in her eyes. If I needed any reward, that was it.

"You want me?" she asked, clapping her hands together.

"Of course we do," Debbie said. "That's why we're here."

I made a mental note to thank Debbie later. She didn't know Mrs. Pulaski very well, didn't love her yet as I did, but because *I* did love her, that was enough for Debbie.

Soon we were both genuinely glad we asked her to stay. It turned out she had some experience with home perms. More than I did, in fact.

"My lady friends," she explained. "We did for each other." She held her nose, and fanned the air. "Ahh, but in those days, the smell! *Phew!*"

"Now," she said, breathing in the perm neutralizer, "smells good."

After the perm was finished, and Debbie's hair had been washed, conditioned, and rolled up neatly, I began on her face, the part I liked best.

Mrs. Pulaski pushed me gently aside. "Wait," she said. "Let me do first."

She made Debbie sit in a comfortable chair and put her head back. With what looked like a homemade cream, she massaged Debbie's skin gently, but firmly with upward, circular movements of her fingers. Debbie was in seventh heaven.

"Oooh, that feels so great," she said. "I'm so relaxed, I could almost go to sleep."

"But your face is awake, yes? It tingles, no?"

"No . . . I mean, *yes*! Feel, Susan, so soft."

"Sometime will you do that to me?" I asked. "I didn't know you could do that."

I was curious about the lotion too. Had Mrs. Pulaski managed to bottle what no one else had? Debbie looked wonderful.

The next part wasn't so wonderful, at least, not for Debbie. She squirmed and "ouched" constantly, as I tweezed the stray hairs that spoiled the line of her eyebrows.

"Be *quiet*," I commanded. "Suffer!" I laughed. "Besides, I never promised you a rose garden."

"Yes, you *did*," she said gasping. "This *hurts*."

But it was over soon enough, and a cold washcloth pressed against the freshly weeded eyebrows calmed her. I waited for a few minutes and then I started with the sheer liquid makeup. I was just getting into the blusher when we heard Mr. Pulaski coming home.

"Sophie?" he called plaintively. "Where are you?"

"Pour the coffee, Stanley," she said. "I am here with the girls."

I couldn't believe it. Meek little Mrs. Pulaski brushing her husband off so nonchalantly.

I was working on the gray eyeliner, and I had to stop for a second to force down a giggle.

Awake was the right word for Debbie's face when I finished. And if her skin tingled, mine did too, with excitement, with pleasure. She looked *beautiful!*

The makeup looked natural, healthy, just right! And her eyes were deeper, more mysterious, the color on her lips and cheeks changing her almost beyond recognition.

No. Not true. It *was* Debbie, but a special Debbie, a *lovely* Debbie.

"Look at yourself," I said, standing her up and turning her toward the big mirror over a bureau.

She let out a long breath, and stared at her reflection.

"Argh-h," she said.

I stared at her. "*What?*"

"Gaaaarg . . ." she said.

I laughed. "You sound like a clogged sink," I said. "Now, *speak*. Tell me what you think."

She found her voice. "Oh, Susan, is that me? *My* face?"

"I told you so," I said smugly.

"My eyebrows look so good," she said wonderingly.

"Keep them that way," I said curtly.

Mrs. Pulaski came over and stood beside Debbie. She put her hands on Debbie's head and for a minute, I thought she was giving her some kind of old country blessing. But no, she was testing her hair for dryness.

"Ah, still wet," she said, sounding very disappointed. "I want to see the hair."

"It will take a while longer, I'm afraid," I said. "It was still pretty damp when I set it."

Mrs. Pulaski straightened her shoulders, and when she spoke, her voice was firm.

"Then you will both stay for supper. We will wait."

She looked at me and then at Debbie. "You will call your mothers. Tell them that Mrs. Pulaski is feeding you on this night."

She patted Debbie on the arm. "When your boyfriend sees you. . . ." Her husky voice sounded dreamy.

"I don't have a boyfriend, Mrs. Pulaski," Debbie said.

"You will, dahling," she said. "Ah, you *will*."

CHAPTER SEVEN

We were all pleased with ourselves, Mrs. Pulaski, Debbie and me; even Mr. Pulaski was pleasant. Mrs. Pulaski told us stories about her girlhood in Poland, and her distinction as "best dancer in the village."

Watching her as she chattered happily, I was reminded of something Grandma Bond told me the year before she died.

"The body changes, the wrinkles come, but in her heart, a small part of every woman is always sixteen."

It was true that night. I had no sense of Mrs. Pulaski as an old woman in her seventies. Her ideas and enthusiasm were as young as mine or Debbie's. In fact, there were moments when I felt older than both of them — almost motherly.

I made a promise to myself then and there to visit Mrs. Pulaski more often and to bring Debbie with me. As much as she loved Katya and no matter how much pleasure the parakeet brought to her life — it was not enough. Katya, after all, is just a bird.

I had a brand-new view of Mrs. Pulaski now. She was like an artist, awaiting the unveiling of her greatest work.

"Is dry now?" she asked eagerly, her hand unable to resist touching the hair still wound tightly on rollers.

I tested Debbie's hair then; it was bone dry.

"Ahhh, so bee-yoo-tee-full," she declared when Debbie's hair was brushed out and combed in place. "So pretty."

It was. Not too curly, just deep, smooth waves, and as advertised, her hair had body now, purpose. It was perfect!

A few more pounds off and some new clothes and Debbie would be completely transformed. I wondered if Debbie would be able to convince her mother that she was capable of shopping for herself.

"What do you think she'll say?" Debbie asked me.

She had been thinking of her mother too; I knew without having to ask who "she" was.

Mrs. Gilmore might hate Debbie's new look. I didn't *know* that, of course; it was perfectly possible that she would be truly pleased to see her only daughter so beautiful, so happy.

I know *I* was very pleased and proud. I was *so* proud of her for her willpower and everything, I wanted to cry.

But I didn't. "Looking good," I said without a trace of emotion. "Looking real good."

She hugged me then, a fast, fierce hug. "Thanks, Susan," she said.

It was just enough; any more and I really would have cried.

The planning stages for the SUPERBALL were long past; the real work lay ahead of us now. Debbie and I, plus the entire decoration committee, spent hours in Mrs. Petrie's artroom. Randy's Batcave was much more than that now. It was going to be a huge, very elaborate underground base for all kinds of superheroes, something representing every one he could think of. There was even going to be a rock (sorry, Randy) displayed under glass: *kryptonite*. Lars Hansen surprised us by designing and painting a really fantastic vehicle that put the Batmobile to shame. And here we thought he was merely a football hero.

Gini Hatch, whose father works for the telephone company, said he was going to borrow an old telephone booth for us to use that night, and Debbie was busy cutting out fancy spiderwebs from black crepe paper.

Debbie and I had also begun a big project with papier mâché: all the planets in the solar system which he would hang from the ceiling, together with blinking, white Christmas tree lights for stars.

I still hadn't decided on a costume. Debbie wanted to be Wonder Woman, but she wasn't sure about it yet. Although she had every reason to feel confident about herself, she was still pretty much the same old Debbie, putting herself down too often. I guess you can change the outside much faster than the inside.

"Wonder Woman wears strapless," she said with a frown. "Can you see me in strapless? I mean, I'm just getting used to the sweaters you helped me choose." She smiled ruefully. "Besides, have you seen the Wonder Woman on TV? Lynda Carter! I certainly can't compete with *her* figure!"

"Who can?" I said. "You don't have to look like Lynda Carter, just interpret the character in your own way."

"How's your mom doing?" I asked her. "Is she over the first shock?"

Debbie had played her homecoming scene for me and she had exaggerated, I'm sure, for humor's sake. But I got the impression Mrs. Gilmore was nervous about Debbie, didn't quite know what to make of her. She wavered between being helpful ("I made a nice salad for you, Debbie") and anxious ("Are you sure you feel all right?"). Still, she had let Debbie use her Ferber's charge. We had a wonderful time, and now Debbie had a good, basic wardrobe of nicely-fitting pants, skirts, and tops. She would buy more when she lost the last pounds, she said.

I loved it the day I saw Joanie Sangerville and Laura Breen look Debbie over with that special, appraising look, that "does she have something I don't have?" look.

For the first time in her life, Debbie was attracting attention. I loved it almost as much as she did. It's a nice feeling to watch someone unfold like that.

It didn't take very long before Mrs. Pulaski's prediction came true. Debbie was delirious with joy and scared to death.

"*I've got a date*," she squealed, clutching at me frantically. A *date*! Susan, with a *guy*!"

"That's good," I said, laughing. "Beats an aardvark."

"No, really, I *mean* it," she said. "He asked me today after Gertie's class. He *waited* for me in the hall. For *me*! Oh, Susan! His name is Michael. Don't you *love* that name?"

"Mmmm, I do," I said, "Mom had a cat named Michael once."

"Suuusan," she wailed. "Be serious. What am I going to *do*?"

"*Do*?" I said, raising my eyebrows high, putting a finger to my forehead. "What *is* the matter, child? Can it be you are not on your mental tip-toes today? You are going to go out with Michael, that's what you're going to *do*!"

"That's what I'll do. I'll go out with him," she said to herself, forgetting all about me. She really was in another world.

"Debbie," I said. "Did you tell him yes?"

"Sure," she said, "The minute after he asked me."

I made a face at her. "Then why are you asking *me* what to do? If you had already decided?"

"I don't know," she said. "I'm not even sure what my name is. Susan, do you realize I'm six-teen years old and this will be the first time I've ever been alone with a guy? I'm so happy and I'm so scared."

"Calm down. *Sit* down, and tell me all about him. Do I know him? Is he new here or what? Tell me from the beginning."

"Okay," she said. "Well, first, he comes from

67

Pennsylvania, some tiny little town in — get this, Susan — The Endless Mountains. He says *Appleby* is city to him."

"Is he a hick?"

"Oh, no, not at all," she said. "He's quite tall and he has this great blond hair, really light blond hair."

Her eyes misted suddenly.

"Susan, he probably had platinum hair when he was a baby."

"Oh, lord," I said, groaning.

"He said he's been dying to ask me out, but he had to check around first to make sure I wasn't already taken. Susan, do you believe that? He thought . . ."

"Of course, he thought," I said, feeling like I was about a hundred years old. "When was the last time you looked in the mirror?"

"Oh, sure, but . . ." she said uncertainly. "I never . . ."

"No," I said evenly, "you've never had a boy interested in you before. But Debbie? I'm sure you do now. Remember? Mrs. Pulaski said it would happen. We'll have to tell her."

But she had stopped listening to me.

"Michael Garrett," she said aloud. "Mi-chael Gar-rett. Debbie Gilmore and Michael Garrett."

I walked away without another word. She wouldn't hear me anyway, I thought, smiling to myself.

CHAPTER EIGHT

"Where are you going with John Saturday night?" Debbie asked me during lunch on Friday.

"The drive-in, probably. John can't stand indoor movies in warm weather. And it really is spring, Debbie. *I* saw my first robin yesterday."

"I know," she said, "I saw a crocus. Susan?"

"What's worrying you?" I asked.

"Well, it's just that . . ."

"I know. I know," I said.

Her eyes opened wide. "How?"

"You're afraid to go out with Michael alone and you want to know if we'll double-date with you."

"Suuusan! You are . . ."

"I know — psychic, brilliant. No, really, I was going to suggest it if you didn't. I've been watching you all week. One minute you're on the tippity top and the next you're in the pits, worrying. Debbie, it's just a date, you know."

"My *first* date," she said. "What will I talk about? How do you talk to a guy?"

"Okay, first tell Michael that we asked you to come with us Saturday night. That will take some of the burden off. It *is* easier the first time if you're with another couple. Second, don't waste all your energy worrying about what to talk about. We're going to the movies, remember?"

She still looked worried.

"All right, so we won't go to the drive-in," I said, unable to hide a smile.

"Well," she said huffily, "I mean — he might think he *has* to kiss me or something."

"Tell you what, I'll ask John if he'll take us to Seaside. We love to do that. It's a nice ride, the boardwalk is fun, and there's a great little place we can go afterward, kind of dark and romantic, yummy Italian food and, get this, *candlelight*."

"Oh, perfect," Debbie said, her face relaxing. "I can just see it now — the ocean breeze riffling through Michael's blond hair, the candlelight on his face."

"Oh, wow," I said. "This guy really has to be something; I can't wait to meet him. The way you talk. . . ."

But she was thinking about something else.

"This place," she said. "Do they serve any diet food?"

"Let up, will you, Debbie? For one night you can forget your diet. You deserve a treat. Besides, how much have you lost so far?

"Fifteen pounds," she said.

"You're fantastic, Debbie," I said. "It didn't take you long at all. You look positively delicate."

Debbie grinned. "Don't say 'delicate' in front of Mom — it will make her nervous."

"I won't. Where'd you get that sweater? I like it."

It was dove-gray, a slipover and it looked good on her.

"It's Mom's. I borrowed it, but don't tell her that either."

I laughed. "Parents usually say, 'My, you're getting so big.' Your parents can't. They have to say, 'My, you're getting so small.' "

"Size seven," she said, half-shy, half-proud.

"Oh, heavens," I said. "I know there'd come a day when I would hate you. Size *seven*! You're too much!"

"No, I'm not. That's one thing I'm not any-more — *too* much."

"You're right, Debs. You're *just* right!"

And she was.

John and Michael hit it off right from the start, especially since Michael insisted on paying for half a tank of gas. John would never have asked him to, but I knew it pleased him. Since John is going to Rutgers College next year, he is banking every possible cent. The Anthonys are pretty well off — John's father owns a construc-tion company — but Mr. Anthony has a thing about not spoiling his kids, making them "too soft." John and his two brothers plus about a half dozen nephews and cousins work part-time in the winter, full-time in the summer. No easy jobs either. They labor right along with the rest of the crew.

Anyway, Michael Garrett was as nice as Debbie said — tall and lean with an impressive thatch of thick, light blond hair. He has the same color eyes that I do, or rather the same mixture of green and yellow and brown — hazel, I guess you say. I had to admit he was very good-looking; although, in my opinion John has him beat. But still, I thought, Debbie and I are doing all right for ourselves, out with two of the best-looking guys in Appleby. I knew she was thinking the same thing. One glance at each other and I felt sure we were in total, blissful agreement.

I sat up front with John naturally, and on the way to Seaside, I could hear the murmur of voices from the backseat, so I settled back and enjoyed the ride. Debbie was doing fine!

It was nice too to be with another couple. It had been a long time since we had. None of my old friends would take a chance on exposing their guys to my influence, old "superflirt" that I am. But Debbie wasn't worried about me; she didn't think like that. Except for Terri Lannigan (who I still like and consider a friend) Debbie is my only friend. I'm fonder of her than any girl I've ever known.

She loved the boardwalk! She was relaxed and able to talk and laugh easily; if I hadn't known better, I would have said it was her hundredth date. She kept us in stitches with her antics ("Step on a crack, you break your mother's back"). Try that on the boardwalk where there is a crack every eight inches. We were a sight, all four of us tiptoeing along trying not to break our mother's backs. And she even did her imitations.

But our moods changed abruptly from rowdy to romantic the minute we entered Lorenzo's. We were shown to a red, cloth-covered table in a quiet corner of the darkened restaurant, and the hyper, hilarious quality of the evening disappeared. Candlelight does work magic, I thought, as I watched the flickering fingers of light touch the faces of my friends. The comparison that came to me was corny maybe, but they seemed to me like Christmas angels.

I wondered what they saw when they looked at me in the same light. Did I have that same soft, ethereal quality?

We all ordered the same thing, spaghetti and meatballs. We were hungry from our boardwalk exertions and besides, it was cheap.

John sang the praises of the garlic bread. "Wait until you taste it. And the best part is they give you seconds, thirds, as much as you want."

John turned to me then and smiled. "Would it be fair to say this is our favorite place, Susan? It's a long ride from Appleby but worth it, well worth it. A great place to take your best girl."

His voice was soft and low, and his eyes were full of love. But for some reason, I wasn't embarrassed, and Michael and Debbie didn't seem to be either. As I said, Lorenzo's is the place for romance, love; a magic place.

Michael opened up too. I could tell he was enjoying himself and was completely at ease with all of us.

"Since I moved here in September, I've been like a hermit or a monk or something, totally cut off from everything and everyone. All my own fault though. I was afraid I'd look like a pushy jerk if I made the first move. So, since no one paid any attention to me, I just made out like I had

73

something very important to do after school every day. Took off like a shot."

He shook his head and laughed. "I got home from school so fast, Mom thought somebody was after me, giving me a hard time. And then, of course, I had nothing to do, so I sat around, being bored, mad at myself and everyone else. I guess my mother is relieved. She was so happy I was going out tonight. I could almost hear her thinking, 'It's about time.'"

He smiled at Debbie. "So I thank you, my mother thanks you, my father thanks you, my sister . . ."

John laughed. "Don't forget to give him his Oscar, Debbie. He sounds like he's making an acceptance speech."

He looked sheepish for a second, then he perked up again. "No, really, if Debbie had turned me down, I don't know what I would have done."

Michael is cute, I thought; the candlelight touches his hair just so and makes it look like the brushed gold I admire so much, a Florentine finish I think it's called. But of course, he wasn't looking at *me*; he had eyes only for Debbie. Not that he totally ignored me; he paid attention when I spoke, laughed if I said something amusing, but as a girl I just wasn't there for him.

I was impatient with myself. Why should that bother me? What did it really matter? John was being his usual sweet, attentive self, and after all, Michael was Debbie's date; naturally his attention would be focused on her. Why did I want him to look at me? Crazy. Stupid. Totally dumb.

But the moment passed thankfully, and I was relaxed again, happy to be at Lorenzo's with my friends. And I was able to be happy for Debbie again. She seemed to be having a wonderful time.

I wasn't wrong. Debbie called me Sunday morning, as early as she dared.

"Susan? I didn't wake your father up, did I?"

"Uh unh," I said. "Don't worry about it."

Usually she worried a lot because she knew *I* did but today talking to me was more important.

"He *kissed* me, Susan — *twice*! And he kisses so *great*! I was so worried about it . . . how to . . . but I think I was *fine*!"

I smiled.

"Are you laughing, Susan? I bet you're laughing at me. Sixteen and the girl's first kiss and all."

"Not laughing, Deb, smiling," I said gently. "I'm just happy for you. Michael's a neat guy."

"Oh, I know, isn't he? Don't you think he's adorable?"

I listened to her, putting in the right words at the right moment. She needed to talk, just as I had needed a sounding board when John asked me out for the first time, when he kissed me, when I realized I was in love. You really need to tell someone, preferably your best girlfriend. Back then, I had Terri who, as I remembered now, had listened and smiled and understood.

Deb sounded like an excited child, so thrilled because of a simple kiss. But I had to remember it was her *first*. She had never had the dubious pleasure of junior high parties and kissing a boy six inches shorter than she was, who was as embarrassed as she was.

75

"Susan, what if he never asks me out again?"

"Oh, stop it, Deb. You heard what he said. He's completely grateful."

"I guess so," she said uncertainly. "I hope he likes me."

I understood, though. Debbie hadn't had time to build up confidence. Good things have to happen enough times before you trust they will keep happening.

"He likes you," I said. "I saw the way he looked at you."

She was off and running again. "Tell me. How did he look at me? Don't leave out any details."

But I covered the phone with my hand, and held it away from my ear.

I heard Dad shouting angrily, and then Mom running up the stairs fast.

"*Sheila.* Get this damn cat out of here. She's got broken glass all over me."

I knew, as Mom must have known, just what had happened. Puddy has a mad passion for dried flowers; apparently she hadn't been able to resist the arrangement beside the bed.

"Debbie? I've got to hang up now. Talk to you later."

"Anything wrong there? Can I help?"

"Wrong?" I said. "What could be wrong in this perfect, all-American home? Everything is just wonderful."

"Oh, Susan," Debbie said, sympathy in her voice. "Listen," she said, "I'm supposed to clean my room, but I'll get out of it. We'll take a walk, do something, talk."

"Thanks, Debbie, I'll see." I hesitated, torn between the desire to run out of the house and away from Daddy's angry voice, or to stay and help Mom pick up the pieces.

"But it depends," I said. "It depends."

CHAPTER NINE

Everything depended on whether or not our house was going to be a place where I could relax, be comfortable, do my homework, wash my hair, help Mom with dinner, have a decent, Sunday-type Sunday. It depended on whether Mom could get through Daddy's tirade, clean up the broken vase, settle him down to sleep, or if she would say something back, *fight* back, in defense of Puddy, herself, me. It depended on whether she could make him understand that, while his life revolved around sleeping, eating, working, and worrying, there were two other people who lived in the house too.

The only word Mom said to him was a mild "relax," but that was all he needed.

"Relax? Relax? How can I relax? I work all night and then I come home to sleep — just to *sleep*, Sheila. Is that too much to ask? Apparently, because then all hell breaks loose, animals all over me, everything crashing around my head plus *there is sun shining in the window*. How am I supposed to sleep with the sun shining in on me like that? I want those shades pulled down!

I sent a bitter message to the sun: Better hide behind a cloud quick. My father hates you.

He came storming down the stairs, pulling on his old brown robe, the robe tie trailing behind him. All he needed now was to trip over it and ...

He did! He didn't fall, but he reeled between the dining room and the kitchen for what seemed like ages, and then to balance himself, he flung out his arms and stood there flapping like a crazed chicken or maybe like a small airplane caught in a thunderstorm.

I laughed. Out loud. I couldn't help it. He looked so darned silly.

In the old days (old days? last year!) Daddy would have laughed too. He might have been sheepish or even pretended to be mad at the world, but he definitely would have enjoyed the joke even if it was on him. Daddy could always laugh.

But right now it was no joke. And he wasn't pretending to be mad; he was *mad*!

"Oh sure, now you," he said, getting red in the face. "On top of everything my own daughter laughs at me. Would you laugh if I had broken my leg, Susan?"

He was glaring at me, his eyes furious. And then his face changed, and he gave me the kind of scornful look he reserves for drunken drivers, or bumbling store clerks, or any person who, for any reason, he can't stand.

I felt myself shriveling inside until I was very small, so small I almost ceased to exist. At that moment, I knew I didn't exist for him. My own father couldn't stand the sight of me. I was just another part of an unfriendly world crashing down around his head.

But I was wrong, wasn't I? Daddy did love me, didn't he? I knew he had loved me once; he had told me so, I had felt it. So what happened? What had I done to make him not love me anymore? He *had* to love me.

"Daddy," I said quickly, following him into the living room. "Don't be mad at me. I'm sorry I laughed. It's just that you looked kind of funny ... *you* know. ..."

Look at me. See me. Tell me you know who I am.

He didn't even turn around.

A thought that I had never let come to the top of my mind came then, hitting me with such a force I wanted to cringe and run away, probably just the way Puddy-Cat did when the vase fell and broke and Daddy yelled.

Maybe Mom and I had been wrong all along; maybe it wasn't the job at Schwaub-Millar that he hated so much, that was making him so unhappy. Maybe he hated *us*, was unhappy with *us*.

If so, what was wrong with me? Had I changed so much? Had Mom changed?

As I stood there, one thing was clear to me: my father had his back turned toward me because ... *he couldn't bear to look at me.*

The same thing had happened with my friends. They hated me too.

But, I thought, there is John, Debbie — they love you. And Mom and Mrs. Pulaski. I tried to think about that. I couldn't be that bad if they loved me.

But strangely, that knowledge didn't help much. Mom, after all, preferred a book and the company of Puddy to me; Mrs. Pulaski was just a lonely old woman, and John was . . . well, as I said, he didn't see anything he didn't want to see. Debbie — my last hope? Sure, she liked me; I was her best friend, but what did she know about people really? She was an innocent, without any experience in judging people. Now that she was pretty, able to strike out for herself, she would see me for what I was. The same way my father did now.

I was still in my pajamas; I hadn't even washed my face yet. Usually on Sundays, I take my time, not getting dressed until almost noon. But now I raced for the bathroom, scrubbed my face, and brushed my teeth with a fierce haste that frightened me. I had to get out of that house.

I dressed quickly, throwing on the first top I touched, the sweater on the top of the pile, the same jeans I had worn the night before. What did I care how I looked?

As I walked past the Pulaski's house, something made me reach up and touch my own cheek. I was crying. The tears were slipping down my cheek, running into my mouth, and I hadn't even known it. There wasn't any lump in my throat, no other sign and feeling of crying — just the tears, big fat tears; the steady, unceasing drip-drip that I couldn't seem to stop. I didn't remember starting to cry either. How stupid, how *weird*, I thought. Stop it, Susan, before someone sees you.

I thought of turning around and walking back

a few yards, up the front steps to Mrs. Pulaski's house, letting her dry my tears, feed me tea and pastry; being her little girl for the rest of the day. But I didn't want to, and besides, why spoil her Sunday?

The same for Debbie. She was so happy today. Let her enjoy it. Why should I bring her my gloom? Oh, I knew she would be all warm and sympathetic, but I didn't want sympathy either; I wanted . . .

But when I asked myself that question — *What do you want, Susan* — I had no answer. And so I walked; listlessly, aimlessly, with no other purpose except to get as far away from my house as possible. The sun was warm on my shoulders, and the sky was the fresh, clean blue of early spring.

I turned right on Damon Road, and when I got to Main Street, I just kept walking, past the pharmacy, past the Methodist Church and the Colonial Bakery. I turned right again and all at once I knew where I was going. I hadn't planned to go to the lake but perhaps something inside me had guided me, turned my aimlessness into purpose, knowing better than I that the lake was a good place, the best place for me.

Appleby Lake could be beautiful; it used to be. I can remember when it was clean and weed-free, and a place for the whole family to go. I learned to swim there, learned to dive, and row, and fish. But now, the wastes from the factories upstream had poisoned it, killed the fish, destroyed not only the life in it, but the life that used to go on around it: family picnics, concerts, small boys delighting in their first batch of tadpoles, or catching their very first fish. It used to be a place for lovers to go too; when I was nine or ten, I used to watch them, sitting on a blanket spread on the grass, their hands, and sometimes their lips, touching.

But still, choked with weeds, the water an evil greenish-brown, the lake welcomed anyone who cared to overlook its ruined beauty, and at this time of year, many did come.

I sat on the grass and watched the family of ducks that swam near the shore. I wondered why they still came here, year after year, despite what had happened to the once pure water. Maybe, I thought, they have nowhere else to go. I wasn't going to think morbid thoughts; I wasn't going to think about anything. I would just make my mind go blank, soak up the sun, let the afternoon go by. People walked by, in pairs, in family groups, talking, laughing. *Who needs them*, I thought. *Who needs anyone?*

"Hey, hiya, Susan, what are you doing down here?"

The sun was in my eyes. I shaded them with my hand, and looked.

His mop of blond hair gave him away before his face was clear. I hadn't recognized his voice. It was deeper today, huskier.

"Michael," I said. "What are you doing here?"

I laughed out loud. For some reason, I was very glad to see him.

"I'm doing this," he said, waving a fishing rod at me.

"Oh, no," I protested. "You don't actually

plan to fish in this glop, do you? It's polluted; no self-respecting fish would be caught dead here!"

He laughed and sat down beside me. "Probably that's what I will catch — a dead fish. I don't know, it's such a great day, I thought fishing sounded like a good idea. Guess I've got spring fever."

"Me too," I said, tilting my head to the side and smiling at him sideways. "But it's no fun having spring fever all by yourself, is it? I know I was just thinking, I wish someone interesting would come along." I paused. "And puff, like magic, *you* came. Lucky me."

He ducked his head and seemed suddenly shy. He didn't say anything.

"Did you have fun last night, Michael?" I asked to break the silence.

He relaxed, and picked at a blade of grass. "Sure did. And as my mother would say, 'It's about time.' I really was in a rut. Talk about lonesome."

"Well, forget about lonesome; you're past that now. We're not going to let you run home every day. That would be a waste, you know, Michael, you're much too good-looking."

He grinned but he looked self-conscious again.

I reached over and patted his hand lightly. "Sorry," I said. "I don't mean to embarrass you. You'll have to get used to me. I say what I think." I paused for a second or two. "That's not quite true, Michael. I *almost* always say what I think. I had the same thought last night at Lorenzo's, but I decided not to say it."

He was looking at the grass.

"Tell me something, now that I've made your face get red, when you were a baby, was your hair platinum blond? I bet it was."

He looked up then, and I gave him my best smile.

"Do I make you uncomfortable, Michael?" I asked softly. "I didn't mean to. I guess I'm just trying to tell you how glad we all are that we met you. How nice we think you are." I gave a small laugh. "I'm saying 'we,' Michael, when I should really only be speaking for myself. I hate people who do that, don't you? Have you ever had a nurse or a teacher who says things like, 'Now, we'll just take your temperature' or 'Now if we'll just do our homework, maybe we'll get an A.' Do you know what I mean? Anyway, when I say we're glad to meet you, I mean me. I'm glad I met you, Michael. I've never known anyone like you."

He had his elbows on his knees and he was holding his chin in his hands. He was looking at me very intently.

"You really do say what you think, don't you, Susan? I envy that. Sometimes I'm so shy it's sickening. I guess that's my biggest problem."

"I think it's important to let people know how you feel about them. And I think, right now, I'm feeling a little unsure of myself too. I mean, I've made it very clear how I feel about you, but I have no idea what you think about me."

He looked confused. "Think? I don't know what you mean."

"You know, Michael. Do you think I'm nice, are you glad you met me?"

I realized I was holding my breath waiting for his answer, and I felt a sudden panic. What was I doing? How could I stoop to asking him that? It wasn't flirting this time. It was something terrible, something desperate. Flirting was a kind of lighthearted, playful pastime; a bit of flattery, along with some words, and looks, and smiles, that combined could win someone's heart, or at the least, their momentary attention. This was serious. And wrong.

"Mmmmm, I'm thinking," he said, looking out across the lake, his chin still in his hands. "But if you want the truth, I really don't know what to say. I'm not a whiz with the words like you are. I told you, I'm shy."

He said the last with a mischievous grin, and suddenly I wasn't afraid anymore. It wasn't obvious that I had been desperate for a sweet word, a compliment. He just had assumed it was my way.

"Shyness sometimes is a copout," I said, making my manner light. "I bet you're really not shy at all. You didn't seem shy last night."

He flopped backward on the grass. "You're right, I wasn't. Maybe it was because we were a group. It's harder talking to a girl alone."

"Oh, come on, Michael, is it really all that hard talking to me? Am I so scary? I don't bite, you know. If there is a local vampire, it's not me, I promise."

After that, the conversation was easier, less of a one-sided thing. We talked about his old hometown, Appleby, ambitions, a family I knew who lived next door to him, parents, and finally, Debbie.

"Where is Debbie today?" he had asked. "Is she meeting you down here?"

"Uh unh," I answered. "She has to stay in and clean her room."

That's really not a lie, I started to tell myself and stopped. *You know it is, Susan — what's the matter with you?*

I pushed away my sense of guilt when he asked me to take a walk with him.

"Just around the lake," he said. "I've been sitting too long, feel like stretching my legs."

So we walked, and talked some more. Except for the vague sense that I was not supposed to be doing this, I was enjoying myself. I had the feeling he was too.

We got around to the subject of the SUPER-BALL.

"It should be fun," I said. "Something different, anyway. Do you think you'll be going?"

"Sure, I'd like to." He hesitated. "Debbie said you two are in charge of it. I guess you'll be going with John, huh?"

"Guess is right," I said without thinking, "He hasn't asked me yet. You know, Michael, sometimes I wonder if it's such a great idea going with the same guy for years and years. You know, it's sort of . . . limiting."

Michael stopped walking and looked at me hard.

"What do you mean, Susan?" he asked quietly.

I swallowed hard. Now I had done it. *Step*

back, Susan, I told myself frantically. *Back out of this gracefully before it's too late.*

But it was too late. Something, someone else had control of my tongue.

"Like now, Michael. Now that I've met you. I wish . . ."

"What do you wish," he asked, looking down at me.

"Michael, did you ever meet someone, just *look* at them and *know*?

"Susan," he said softly.

I whirled and walked away from him. "I'm sorry," I said. "My big mouth — I have no right."

Suddenly I was very frightened. What had I done? I had pulled every trick in the book, had come on stronger than I ever had in my life. I even amazed myself. And he was interested. I could tell by the look in his eyes, the way his face had softened. Now he was beside me, and he put a hand on my waist and turned me to face him.

"Why don't you have any right to like me?" he asked. "Because you're John's girl?"

I felt tears sting my eyes. "Yes," I said miserably. "And because of Debbie. She's your girl, not me."

"What? Are you kidding? Susan, I only went out with Debbie once. Sure, I had a great time and I like her a lot but who said she's my girl? I don't work that fast."

But I do, I wanted to tell him, *I do and I am so ashamed of myself.*

He put a hand under my chin and tilted my

face up toward his. For a split second I thought he was going to try and kiss me.

"Michael," I pleaded.

"Don't worry," he said. "We'll work it out — you'll see. We can have things just the way we want them."

"Listen, Michael," I said, and my voice was tight with fear. "Please just forget I said anything. Forget this whole afternoon. I don't want to hurt anyone. Please. Just chalk it up to the fact that I do have a careless tongue. I talk too much."

"You were only being honest, Susan," he said. "I don't call that careless."

"Please," I said, wanting to end it. "*Just forget it.* You're a really nice guy and I like you but. . ."

"And I like you too. I have to confess something — I thought you looked so beautiful last night with the candlelight and all. I never would have told you that except . . ."

I was really in a panic now. "Thanks, Michael but listen, we're just friends, you know. That's all it can ever be."

"I understand, Susan. You're a nice girl and a very loyal friend. I can see how you feel about hurting other people and I admire that. But you said it — when you meet someone and you *know*."

I had to get away from him. He wasn't listening to me anymore. I had put these romantic ideas in his head, and now he was really getting into it, enjoying it thoroughly.

I tried to smile. "Remember now, just friends." I turned to leave, and then turned back to him.

"Pretend this afternoon never happened, Michael. Please, as a favor to me. Believe me, it will be much better that way."

He smiled back at me, a soft tender little smile, and for an instant, I was caught between a feeling of utter satisfaction and complete disgust with myself.

On the way home, I remembered the conversation I had had with Debbie. Life was so simple once — the stove was hot and the freezer was cold. The truth was the truth and a lie was a lie. And then I had gone on with some crazy spider theory, talking about how complicated life had become. *Baloney!* I thought now.

The sun had gone behind a cloud and I was shivering as I walked. Baloney because life was still simple when you got right down to basics. The fire was hot, and the truth was still the truth. And the truth was today I had played with fire and almost gotten burned. No more, I vowed. I'm never going to do that again. Playing with fire was just too dangerous and I was afraid of it now.

CHAPTER TEN

"Sorry I yelled at you, Susan," Dad said.

He was sitting in his recliner, the Sunday papers on his lap. He was dressed for a change; I could tell he had shaved and showered. His mood had improved a lot, but his apology was said so casually, I knew he didn't consider his behavior earlier any big deal.

No big deal to *you* maybe, I thought bitterly. And it didn't help matters when he calmly picked up a section of the paper and began to read. I was dismissed.

"S'okay," I mumbled and kept on going.

Mom was in the kitchen peeling potatoes. I fell in beside her at the sink, and began rinsing, then quartering the potatoes.

"What else are we having?" I asked. The oven was on.

"Very unexciting," she said. "Chicken. But I did make the stuffing you like. We'll eat about five."

I put the cut potatoes in a heavy pot, added some water, and placed them on the back of the stove.

"Anything else I can do now?" I asked. I could

see she had things under control; vegetables would come later, and I would set the table.

Suddenly she was hugging me. I returned her hug automatically, but my surprise made me stutter.

"Wh-h-at?"

"Oh, Susan Bee," she whispered fiercely. "I'm so sorry. I wish . . ."

I pulled back and looked at her. There were tears welling in her eyes, and her face was pale and tired-looking. I felt a strong urge to keep on holding her, to comfort her, but mixed with that feeling was an angry impatience. Shape up, I wanted to say. I wanted to ask her the questions that bothered me so: What is the matter with Daddy? What is the matter with you? Why is he so ugly and why are you so wishy-washy? Most of all, I wanted to ask the question that had sent me running out of the house earlier: Is it my fault?

She was saying something now. "Please don't worry, it will be better soon."

"I'm not worried, Mom," I said breezily, moving out of her arms. I made a silly face. "Do I *look* worried?"

"Susan . . ."

"Call me when you need help with dinner," I said and left the kitchen quickly before she could say anything else.

Debbie wasn't in school on Monday. It didn't worry me too much; if she was sick, I didn't think it could be anything serious; I had talked to her yesterday and she was fine.

In one way, I was relieved. I still hadn't figured out what to do, or what to say to her. It might be better to say nothing, just be extra nice. What I had done yesterday had nothing to do with our friendship, I thought. I hadn't planned or wanted to hurt her. None of the other girls could understand that; *I didn't want to hurt anyone.*

A good night's sleep had done me a lot of good; I felt better today, stronger, not so scared or worried. After all, I thought, no real harm has been done. And I had learned my lesson — *no more flirting.* At least not when I was in that reckless kind of mood, not when I was upset and angry. It always seemed to turn into something else then.

I would call Debbie when I got home. I decided I would mention that I saw Michael at the lake, fishing. If I didn't mention it and *he* did, then it would look funny; she would wonder about it.

But when I called her later, her mother said she was sleeping and couldn't come to the phone.

"What's the matter with her, Mrs. Gilmore?" I asked. "Is she sick?"

I thought she hesitated for a long time. "She's not feeling well, Susan," she said. "I'm not sure what's wrong."

"Do you think she'll be in school tomorrow?" I asked.

"I'm not sure," she said.

Mrs. Gilmore's voice sounded funny, quivery, and she didn't hang up right away. It was as if she wanted to say something more, or maybe waiting for *me* to say something.

"Well, thank you for calling, Susan. Good-bye."

I said good-bye and put the phone down. Something was wrong; I had a funny feeling in my stomach, an uneasy feeling. I forced myself to get up, walk around, trying to shake off the feeling that Debbie wasn't sick at all, that she was standing right there by the phone, that her mother had lied for her, that *she just didn't want to talk to me*.

That's stupid, I told myself. It's what happens when you feel guilty about something; you start imagining things. Maybe Debbie really was sick — a virus can knock you down in a matter of hours — or maybe Debbie had an argument with her parents, or maybe there was some problem at home that she hadn't told me about. Anyway, I thought, Debbie will probably be in school tomorrow. If it had been a scene with her mother, I was sure Debbie would act it out for me the way she always did. I would laugh, the way I always did. The air would be clear again, our world would be right. Suddenly, I couldn't wait for tomorrow. I really wanted to see Debbie.

But she wasn't in school Tuesday. I called her again and this time Steve answered. All he said was, "I'll tell her you called," and then hung up on me. He didn't sound strange though, just hurried. Maybe something really was going on in the Gilmore household.

On Wednesday I did start to worry again. The least she could do was give me a quickie call. She couldn't be that sick.

After school I went to the artroom and spent

about an hour painting planets. It wasn't any fun, though, without Debbie there to be silly with. Always before, working on the dance was like playing. Today, it just seemed like work.

Mrs. Petrie wasn't in the room either which was unusual; she always stayed there with us, at least until four. But just as I was gathering up my books, ready to leave, she returned.

"Oh, Susan. Good, I caught you before you left. Could I speak to you for a moment?"

She had a slip of paper in her hand and she had a puzzled look on her face.

"Do you have any idea why Debbie Gilmore is resigning as co-chairperson for the dance?" She tapped the paper with her index finger. "Or why she is transferring out of my class?"

She was looking at me, waiting for my response and I could only stare back at her.

"I have a note from the office here. It was in my mailbox. Apparently Mrs. Gilmore called school and arranged for these changes with Debbie's guidance counselor. 'For Personal Reasons' the note says."

I didn't know what to say.

"Susan, you're her best friend so you must know what's wrong. Did I do something? Did she dislike me?"

Mrs. Petrie was very upset.

"I just don't understand it," she said. "Everything seemed to be going so well for her. She was . . . she *seemed* happier, and, of course, she lost all that weight and looked so wonderful."

"I don't know, Mrs. Petrie," I said honestly. "The last time I talked to her was Sunday. Her mother just said she wasn't feeling well when I called Monday. And Tuesday, her brother brushed me off."

"Well, it's really a mystery," she said. "I don't know what to think. If I did anything . . ."

"No, Mrs. Petrie," I said as firmly as I could. "I know Debbie likes you a lot. This was her favorite class."

"Susan, do me a favor, will you? If you talk to her, if there is anything I can help her with, will you let me know? I feel bad about this because I like Debbie very much."

I gathered up my books, and moved toward the door. "I will," I said. "I'll try to find out today."

I thought about it all the way home, and a feeling of real dread had taken over by the time I reached Appleby Square. It had to have something to do with me; certainly Mrs. Petrie had nothing to do with Debbie's resignation or class transfer. I had to think it: Art was the only class Debbie and I had together, plus working on the dance meant working with *me*. It explained why she wouldn't talk to me on the phone, why she wouldn't even come to school.

But it didn't seem possible. It was too . . . *crazy*. Even if someone had seen me talking or walking with Michael on Sunday, would Debbie jump to conclusions like that? Would she take someone else's word for it, for *whatever*?

Unless Michael . . . No, I thought, of course not. I had told Michael very plainly: forget it. He wouldn't be that dumb.

Instead of going home, I headed for the Gilmores' house. No matter what happened, I had to find out if Debbie was all right. Something was definitely very wrong.

Mrs. Gilmore answered the door. Her thin face was even more anxious than usual; she almost pulled me in the door.

"Susan, *please* tell me what's going on. I'm so worried about Debbie and she won't tell me anything. She's been so strange since Sunday night ever since that boy came over. Susan, do you know anything? Did that boy say something, do anything to hurt her? She won't talk to me. I'm at my wit's end."

Since that boy came over. Michael? Oh, no!

"Monday morning she came downstairs and told me to call the school. She told me to get her out of the art class and her dance activities. She said if I didn't she would quit school completely. Susan, *Debbie is an A student.*"

Her shoulders slumped and she dabbed at her eyes.

"What could he have done to her? She even looks different now. She hasn't used any of the new makeup, and she pulls her hair back with a rubber band. She's completely lost interest in her appearance. I just don't know."

She looked at me pleadingly. "Talk to her, Susan. Find out what's troubling her. I know she'll talk to *you*; you're her best friend. She *trusts* you."

"I'll do what I can, Mrs. Gilmore," I said. "Where is she?"

"In her room," she said sadly. "She's *always* in her room."

I felt strange — cold, almost numb — and on the way upstairs, I kept hearing Mrs. Gilmore's voice. *She trusts you,* Susan. There was no doubt in my mind anymore; *I* had done this to Debbie. She hadn't had time or experience enough to build up any tough skin, so she was open, vulnerable to everything. A baby bird, newly out of the nest, just learning how to fly.

I stood silently outside her closed door and tried to gather my thoughts, my strength. I had played with fire, and had felt lucky because I had escaped the flames, and felt virtuous because I had promised never to do it again. But the flames had touched Debbie. I took a deep breath as I put my hand on the doorknob. Please, Debbie, I prayed silently, please, just *listen.*

She was sitting in her director's chair, the one she loved so much because she had covered it herself with a sunny yellow canvas, her favorite color. She had her feet up on the windowsill, and her hands were folded in her lap. The window shade was pulled down only a little bit, and she could have been looking out the window, but I saw that she wasn't. Her gaze was directed to the right of the window: *she was staring at the blank wall!*

I hadn't knocked on her door. I knew she wouldn't let me in if I had.

"Debbie," I said very, very softly. "It's me, Susan."

She turned then, and I sucked in my breath, trying to prepare for an angry face, a face filled with loathing, to hear the worst words she could think of.

But her eyes were dull, the color of mud, impossible because Debbie's eyes are a rich, dark blue. Her hair was pulled back just as her mother had said, with a rubber band, but so tightly the corners of her eyes seemed stretched, and the high cheekbones which had been her pride and joy stood out prominently. She looked like a person who had been very sick for a long time.

"Oh, Debbie," I whispered. "I'm so sorry."

There could be no denials, no excuses. *She knew.* There was absolutely no doubt in my mind that she knew exactly what I had done, what I had said to Michael by the lake. But what she didn't know probably was that I had realized what I was doing, had *stopped*, had told Michael to forget it.

"I want to tell you, Debbie, it didn't mean anything. It doesn't mean that I've stopped being your friend. I wasn't out to hurt you, I *never* would hurt you deliberately. It's something else, you see, it's something I can't help. . . ."

"No," she said, her voice as flat and as dull as her eyes. "I know you can't help it. If you could do that to me right after you heard me babbling over the phone about Michael kissing me, heard how happy I was. . . ."

"I didn't *mean* to, Debbie. *Please. Listen.*"

She was quiet; she appeared to be waiting.

"Michael should never have . . ." I began.

"Should never have what? Tattled on you? He should have known better, right, Susan? I mean, how dumb. Proves he *is* a hick, doesn't it? How unsophisticated he is, he thought he had to come over and explain to me why he wouldn't be asking me to the dance, and why he wouldn't be asking me out again.

"Not that he had actually *promised* to call; I even was afraid he wouldn't, remember? And not that he had already asked me to the SUPERBALL either; we had just talked around the subject. So, really, he didn't owe me a thing, did he? You always told me how good John is, how *decent* he is, so honest, and fair, and cheerful about everything. And there were two ways you would talk about it, about him. Sometimes you were bragging, other times you were complaining. I thought maybe you kind of looked down on him for being so unrealistic, so dumb.

"Well, Michael is just like John in that way. He's too honest for his own good. If he was smart, he could have had *both* of us. And I wouldn't have suspected a thing. I never believed all those stories about you. I figured those girls were jealous of you because you had more than they did. I thought it was great that you knew how to talk to boys, and make them like you. And of course, you did so much for me, you were just like my fairy godmother or something."

I could see that she was going to keep right on talking; there would be no stopping her. She had been thinking of nothing else since Sunday. But I couldn't let her talk and not listen to me.

"Debbie, whatever Michael told you, I won't say it isn't true. I think you're right — he is honest and he means well. But did he tell you that I changed my mind, that I stopped . . ."

The expression on her face stopped me. Now she did look angry.

"Well, maybe *you* stopped, maybe you decided *you* don't want *him*, but he hasn't stopped. As he said, 'Sometimes, love just happens that way. You look at someone and you know.' Does that sound familiar, Susan? And oh, how he admires you. He thinks you're the greatest thing since . . . oh, I don't know what. 'She doesn't want to hurt you, Debbie,' he said, 'or John either.' And get this, Susan, he reminded me again just before he left, Susan is your best friend — don't hold this against her."

"It's true, Debbie," I said. "I *am* your friend. I wasn't saying that to be noble or to look good in Michael's eyes. I realized what I was doing and I told him to forget it, to forget everything I said. You've got to believe me!"

"You don't want Michael then?" Her voice was so soft, almost a whisper.

"No, Debbie, no!"

She sat forward suddenly, swinging her legs from the windowsill in one swift motion. Her face was very close to mine and her eyes were blazing. This wasn't Debbie, not the Debbie I knew. And she wasn't some poor, helpless little baby bird, unable to fend for herself. This was a strong person, very sure of herself, very tough. Suddenly I was frightened.

"Do you know what *I* want, Susan?"

I couldn't move; I just stared at her, not answering.

"*I want you to get out of my room.*"

Each word was deliberate, hard and biting.

"I want you to get out of *my house.*"

She hesitated for only a fast beat of my heart.

"I never want to see you or talk to you again."

I was a dumb thing, just standing, staring at her. I was trembling. Had I done this?

She turned her face to the window. When she spoke again, her voice had lost its hard edge; she just sounded very tired.

"And you don't have to worry either," she said. "I'm not going to stay in my room forever. I don't plan to be some weirdo hermit. I hate to worry Mom, you know how it is."

I guess I didn't move fast enough.

"Get out," she said, not turning around. "Get out of here and leave me alone."

I ran then. Ran down the stairs, past Mrs. Gilmore, and out the back door. I heard her calling me, but I didn't stop. I didn't stop running until the pain in my side forced me to slow down to a walk.

My house was quiet and dim as usual. For the first time, I was glad for it. And I understood too, why Mom has to hide out in her room. Sometimes, when things get to be more than you can handle, and the pain gets too bad, it's all you can do.

CHAPTER ELEVEN

Michael came over after supper. Mom let him in and then called me down from my room. She gave me a funny look before she left us alone, as if to ask, "Who's this?" I felt like shouting at her, "There's a lot of things you don't know about!"

I didn't want to talk to Michael, but before I could say a word, he launched into a detailed account of how he felt about me, what he had said to Debbie, and the wonderful times ahead of us. And then, to make a *real* impression on me, he described his conversation with *John*!

"I want everything straight," he said earnestly. "I thought John was a great guy and I'd like us all to remain friends, if possible."

I knew right then for sure that I had really lost it all: Debbie, John, and even Michael. I had told Debbie the truth. I didn't want Michael as a boyfriend. Now it was impossible to have him even as a friend. Plus (maybe this isn't fair) I resented his blundering, his interference in my life. By taking care to make everything "straight," he had ruined three lives; counting his, maybe four.

No, I really *wasn't* being fair. It was my fault, and I couldn't blame Michael.

"What did John say?" I asked. Did I really want to hear?

"He seemed kind of shocked at first," Michael said. "I told him how we felt about each other, and that you were all upset because you didn't want to hurt him. I explained that I wasn't a sneaky kind of guy, that I didn't want to go behind his back or anything. And that you didn't either."

"Go on," I said. I tried to imagine the scene but I couldn't. It was hard for me to believe Michael had actually said those things.

"But then he seemed okay; he was pretty low-key, in fact. He just said, 'Go to it, Michael — she's all yours.' "

I thought this afternoon had made me immune to everything, but I was wrong. It hurt.

"Oh, Michael," I said, putting my face in my hands.

"Come on now, Susan," he said soothingly. "You don't have to worry. Everything's all fixed up. And it wasn't that hard; like I said, John was cool about it, and Debbie too. They didn't get mad or anything. You know, maybe John might be relieved. You said yourself it's a mistake to limit yourself to one person for so long; maybe he was feeling the same way.

He was completely unaware of the fact that every word he said was making it even more terrible than it was before. I wanted him to stop, to shut up, to leave me alone. I wanted to yell, as Debbie had, '*Get out of my house,*' but I didn't.

"Please go home now, Michael," I said as gently as I could.

He was crouching beside me then, pulling my hands away from my face, looking up into my face.

"I don't get it, Susan. Aren't you glad?"

"*Glad*?" I said, choking out the word. "Oh, Michael, it's *awful*!"

I couldn't help it; I started to cry.

"What's the matter?" he said, his face troubled. "This is what you wanted, isn't it, Susan? Now we can go out, go to the dance together, and no hard feelings with anyone."

"You don't know what you're talking about," I cried. "You've got everything all wrong. Michael, I was lying to you. I was *playing* with you."

He crouched there, but he seemed frozen.

"*Playing?* What do you mean, *playing*?"

"Playing," I said. "Like a cat with a mouse, or a spider luring the poor innocent little fly into her web. *That* kind of playing."

Let him hate me so much he'll go running back to Debbie. They can have a wonderful time hating me together.

"You're new in Appleby, Michael," I said. "So you probably haven't had time to hear all the gossip. If you hadn't run home every day, you might have been prepared for me, for all my *tricks*. I'm famous, you know, or I guess the right word is *infamous*. I take my friends' guys away from them. I've done it lots of times.

"Go back to Debbie, Michael," I said, watching him as he got up, and walked toward the front door. She won't hold all this against you, I don't think."

The disgusted, scornful look on his face almost stopped me. I hated anyone to look at me like that. He opened the door, walked out, and shut it quietly behind him.

Daddy? Do you appreciate that? He could have slammed the door and ruined your sleep. I laughed, but it wasn't really a laugh. I don't know what it was.

And then the tears came again, but softly, slowly. I walked upstairs, and went to my room. I sat on the edge of my bed for a long time, not thinking, not even really sad or upset anymore. What was the use? It was all over now, at least for me.

It was only eight-thirty, but I decided to go to bed, hopefully to sleep. Maybe in my dreams something nice would happen.

Puddy scratched at my door and I let her in. Puddy is Mom's cat really, but she is a democratic animal, giving us all equal time. It may be my imagination, but every time I feel bad, Puddy is always there, always seems to *know*. At those times, she is very affectionate, and though I can't prove it, she has a worried look in her big yellow eyes.

Whether or not I imagine Puddy's ESP powers, I was very glad to see her. I patted the bed and she jumped up. Though I pulled the covers up so she could make a nest the way she liked to do, she ignored that and settled on my stomach instead.

I don't care what anyone says, she *did* look concerned.

"Oh, Pud," I said, stroking the velvety black fur. "Everything is rotten. I really made a mess of things this time."

I was surprised at how calm my voice was because, inside, I could feel myself getting panicky. It was all beginning to hit me again, and I kept having flashbacks: Debbie's tight face, Michael's scornful one. I could only guess at how John's face looked when he told Michael, "Take her; she's yours!"

But, I thought, John doesn't know the whole story. He only heard Michael's version.

"What do you think, Puddy? Do I dare call John? Do you think he'll talk to me?"

Maybe if I appealed to his sense of fairness, or told him Michael had exaggerated, even made the whole thing up.

But I knew I couldn't do that.

"I can't lie to him, Pud. That would be the worst insult."

Puddy looked at me steadily, blinking her eyes every so often. Was she agreeing with me? At least she was sitting still for me, and she *seemed* to be listening.

Even if I had to accept the fact that my friendship with Debbie was over and that she really never wanted to see me or talk to me ever again, and Michael Garrett felt the same way, should I just accept Michael's word that John hadn't cared very much one way or another? Shouldn't I at least try to find out?

If only I could win John back. If I could just

make him understand me as I really was, not as he had *thought* I was. I let myself dream about it: John taking me back, John *loving* me again.

I got out of bed, and opened the door, leaving Puddy on the covers, stretching, to wait for me. Mom and Dad were downstairs; I could hear them talking. I went into their bedroom and sat down on the side of the bed where the phone was.

Please, John, I prayed silently as I dialed his number, please love me enough to listen.

Mr. Anthony answered the phone, and when he heard my voice, he made a harumping sound. John's father is the strict, macho type. I don't think he likes the fact that girls can call boys now.

Then John was saying hello, and I could feel my heart thudding against my chest, the way it does when I'm very frightened.

I *was* scared. Everything depended on this call.

"Hi, John," I began, and then afraid he would simply hang up on me, I hurried. "Just listen to me for a minute. You don't have to say anything. Just listen, *please*."

"Hey, Susan," he said wearily, "I don't want to hear anything."

"But you don't know, John . . ."

"I know, Susan. I guess I've known for a long time."

"Please," I pleaded.

"I've got to go," he said. "We're on our way out to dinner. It's my Dad's birthday."

"Will you call me later? Or maybe come over? I don't care what time. We've got to talk, John."

"No we don't," he said. "Or at least I don't.

There's nothing I want to say to you." He paused for a second. "Except good-bye. I guess that's the only thing I want to say to you."

I heard myself moan. "Don't say that, please. You have to let me explain."

I heard the click and I knew he had hung up. I sat holding the phone against my ear, not believing what had just happened.

It wasn't *what* he had said. I could believe that. It was the *way* he said it, so cool, so uncaring.

I put down the phone carefully, and went back to my room and crawled into bed, grateful for Puddy's warmth. Because my hands were suddenly very cold. *I* was cold.

John has few faults, in fact, none that I know of. One trait, which I always thought of as proof of his strong character, was the way he made decisions and stuck to them. Once his mind was made up, he never wavered. It had never occurred to me that it was not just a trait, that it *could* be a fault.

But now it hit me hard. John was stubborn, very stubborn. If he had said good-bye, then that was it for me. I didn't have a chance.

CHAPTER TWELVE

It was crazy, but at the lowest point of my life, things were improving at home. I was walking around on the verge of tears most of the time while, incredibly, Mom and Daddy were laughing and talking more than they had in months.

Daddy woke in a good mood, full of energy and plans. Mom was taking a new interest in almost everything; she looked cheerful, brighter, prettier.

I'd come in from school, and there they'd be, talking, smiling at each other, joking around.

It was terrible. I couldn't stand it.

I suppose if everything wasn't so horrible for me, I'd be happy for them, accept it all without question. I might even start believing in miracles. But I *was* questioning it; what was going on? What had happened? I even asked Mom a few times but all she said was, "When things get too bad, they just have to get better."

Maybe there is some kind of rule, or principle: a family takes turns being miserable. First Daddy, then Mom, then me, then all together. Right now, it was going in reverse order or something. I seemed to be the only miserable one.

At school, it was deadly. No one *said* anything

but I felt as if everyone was talking about me behind my back. It was possible one of the three — Michael or Debbie or John — had told the story about me. It wasn't something I *thought* they would do, but I couldn't be sure.

And Mrs. Petrie was nagging me.

"Did you find out anything, Susan? Have you talked to Debbie?"

"No," I said and didn't explain. What was I supposed to say?

She was still bugging me about it on Thursday. Finally I told her.

"It's not you she's mad at, Mrs. Petrie. She hates me."

I didn't say why.

She looked thoughtful, and rather sad.

"That's too bad, Susan. You were working so well together and were such good friends. I really hope you'll be able to work things out."

"Oh, sure," I said. "It's just one of those things."

She nodded. "Even close friends don't always see eye to eye. But when two people really care about each other, they usually find a way to solve their problems. True friendship, like love, doesn't always run smooth."

I smiled, thanked her, and walked away. She couldn't know how far off the track she was. There was no way to solve our problem because it wasn't a problem at all. It was more like a disaster, so total that there is nothing left to save. All that Debbie and I had built together, all the trust, loyalty, and enjoyment had been destroyed, and just like Humpty Dumpty, it couldn't be put back together again.

I stayed after school and worked on the decorations, kept track of ticket sales, and supervised the refreshment plans. Everything was coming along fine but all the joy had gone out of it for me. It was just work, but I was glad for it; it helped to pass time. Like Debbie had said at the beginning the SUPERBALL was "a laugh and a half" to me. I wouldn't be going.

Probably Debbie wouldn't be going either. All the dieting, the makeover, what good was it now? I had spoiled it for both of us.

My old "friend" Joanie Sangerville must have had her radar working overtime or else she had heard the whole story. I didn't know that for sure, but Joanie zeroed in on me like a bee on clover.

"What's the matter with your friend, Debbie?" she asked after third period on Friday. "She looks awful."

I hadn't seen Debbie up close although I knew she was in school. A few times I had caught a glimpse of her ahead of me, in the halls, or in the lunchroom.

"What do you mean, awful?" Had something else happened to her? Was she really sick or what?

"Oh, I don't know," she said, shrugging. "Pale, blah, all washed out. And just recently we were all saying how good she looked."

When I didn't answer right away, she gave me a shrewd look.

"Haven't you even seen her, Susan? I thought you two were best friends."

She hovered over me, reminding me so much of a bee, I almost expected her to buzz. I wondered if she had her stinger ready.

She did.

"Or did something happen? Maybe you're not friends anymore?"

I just made a face and walked away from her.

All the way home from school, I thought about Debbie. The last thing I wanted to happen was for her to stop caring about herself. It hadn't been just her appearance that had changed for the better, it was her whole attitude, her whole life.

When I got home, I was very restless. The whole weekend loomed ahead and there was nothing, absolutely nothing, to look forward to. Still, though I knew I couldn't be all smiley and cheerful at home, I determined to at least keep my troubles to myself.

Mom and Daddy were sitting at the kitchen table, sipping wine out of the good glasses, their faces all lit up like they had won the lottery or something. And, in fact, there was a sheet of impressive looking stationery on the table in front of them. As a final touch, although it was just past three in the afternoon, Mom was all dressed up in her red silk party pajamas.

"Oh, Susan Bee," she said, spotting me. "Honey, I'm so glad you're home. We're celebrating; we have such wonderful news for you."

"What is it?" I said, hoping I would be able to

work up enough enthusiasm to satisfy them. What could be so great?

"Here, read this," Mom said, handing me the letter. I glanced at the letterhead ...

Benson & Benson Health Products, Inc.
One Thirty Benson Way
New Brunswick, New Jersey

... and then at the signature:

Charles Purcell Benson
Vice-President

I scanned the body of the letter quickly.

". . . very pleased . . . offer you . . . General Manager . . . Southwood plant. Effective May 3 . . ."

I was stunned. This *was* big news!

"How did this happen?" I said excitedly. "I didn't even know you were looking for a new job."

"Isn't it great? Susan?" Mom said. "Aren't you proud of your father?"

"Wow, General Manager. And you'll be the boss at Southwood?" I asked.

He couldn't hide his pleasure anymore. "A regular Big Shot I am," he said, grinning broadly.

"Actually, Suse, the Southwood plant is Benson & Benson's smallest, and my duties won't be too different from what I was doing at S-M, except . . ." he paused, and leaned back in his chair, and flicked an imaginary cigar, ". . . I have a rather large office *and* a secretary, and — get this, you two — my own coffee machine."

Mom laughed happily. "The coffee machine I approve of. What does your secretary look like?"

"A Cheryl Ladd type, *very* distracting," Dad said with a straight face.

"Oh, *really*?" Mom said, trying to look annoyed but failing miserably. I knew even if Daddy's secretary *was* Cheryl and Suzanne Somers all rolled up in one, Mom wasn't one bit worried. Nothing could bring her down today.

"Our worries are over," she said, sighing blissfully. "Just think, Susan, we'll be able to live like normal people again. No more whispering, no more walking around on little cat's feet. We can talk out loud, sing, *entertain*."

I knew our ESP was working again when we both said "Thank heavens" at the same time.

Daddy looked sheepish.

"I guess I have been a bit of a grouch," he began.

"*You said it!*" Mom and I said in unison.

"Hard to live with," he said.

"Impossible," Mom said.

"Horrible," I said. "*Really* awful."

"The third shift was the pits," Daddy said. "The company wouldn't make any improvements; management was so tight they squeaked. The men complained to me and when I tried to reason with the brass, I got chewed up and spit out, and sent back to report to my men empty-handed. Every night it was complain, yell, fight. I was smack in the middle, helpless. Plus I kept thinking I had to hold on to the job no matter what. I was forty-two years old. Who else would hire me?"

"Benson & Benson, that's who," Mom said. "I told you."

"Susan, your mother deserves all the credit. If she hadn't issued an ultimatum, told me to shape up or else, I never would have dared to apply for this job. She lit a fire under me. She even had the nerve to wake me up, put the phone in my hand, and licked the stamps on all the letters I sent out. A very strong lady, your mother, when she finally decides enough is enough."

I had to grin. It was one of her favorite expressions, one I loved to hear.

I was happy for him, for them, and even for myself. I had only one regret. I wished Benson & Benson had a plant somewhere about three thousand miles away from Appleby. My only chance was to be somewhere where no one knew me, a brand-new start.

I sat with them a while longer. I kept a smile on my face, and tried to sound just as thrilled as they did, but after a while, I was aware of a feeling that I recognized as resentment. Traitorous thoughts, like evil toads, kept popping into my head: "I'm glad you two are happy, now that you've messed up *my* life" or "It's all very nice but where were you when I needed you?"

It got worse. The anger began to boil in me like a witches' brew, and the toads were only one ingredient.

I couldn't stop it no matter how hard I tried. If I didn't get away from them, I would scream, and it wouldn't be "whoopee."

I practically ran from the room.

116

Apparently they hadn't noticed my change of mood, because on my way up the stairs, I heard Mom's laughter, and Daddy's hearty, party voice asking, "How about it? More wine, sweetheart?"

CHAPTER THIRTEEN

In the morning Mom made a quick inventory of Daddy's closet and decided he needed an update on his wardrobe. One ten-year-old suit and two sport jackets were not enough for "a man in your position," she told him. She had him out the door and on the way to Ferber's before he could say much more than, "Hey, Sheila, at least let me tie my shoes."

She was excited and determined, and I knew there would be no stopping her in that mood. I didn't think Daddy would fight it very much; I could tell he was excited too. I even heard him mention Victoria Station as a possibility for lunch. I was sure they would have a very nice day together.

They hadn't invited me. Not because they didn't want me, or because they were being thoughtless; I knew it just didn't occur to them. They assumed a sixteen-year-old girl would have better things to do on a Saturday.

But I didn't. Not one thing. I thought about going next door to visit Mrs. Pulaski, but that didn't appeal to me. In fact, nothing appealed to me. My room needed vacuuming, I had sweaters to handwash, and my nails were a mess. I couldn't seem to work up enough energy or interest for any of it. Was I depressed because I was tired, or was I tired because I was depressed? I was tired *and* depressed, I decided, and bored.

I wandered around the house listlessly and then finally dragged myself over to the couch. It wasn't a bit cold in the house but I covered myself up with the blue wool afghan anyway. If somebody walked in now, I thought, they would swear I was sick. I *was* sick — of myself.

Mom's magazines were stacked neatly on the shelf beneath the coffee table. Mom reads everything; her interests range from archaeology, food, and fashion, to science-fiction, psychology, and organic gardening. She also reads everything written about Egypt.

I glanced through the pile of magazines with a half-hearted hope I would spot something that interested me enough to read; anything to pass the hours ahead of me.

I had to smile though when I saw the April issue of *Slim 'n' Trim* magazine. I picked it up and a small booklet titled "Calorie Counting Made Easy" dropped out. So Mom had started dieting again. It was a very good sign; it meant she was happy with herself again. Not that she ever needs to lose that much; usually it's a matter of five or six pounds.

I've never had a weight problem, but before I knew it, I found myself reading an article written by a woman who had lost one hundred and ten pounds in a year.

"For years I have been carrying around an extra person, and 'she' was heavy . . ." she wrote.

She explained how she reduced successfully without a formal diet plan.

"It was just a matter of getting to know myself, learning how, when, and why I ate so much. The 'why' was the most important question."

I glanced at the Before photo. She was a lumpy, dumpy, unhappy-looking woman. Next to that picture was a radiant, smiling, slim beauty. It was amazing.

I had just decided not to finish the article (what did it have to do with me?) when one sentence almost jumped off the page at me. The sudden shock of recognition made my heart beat faster.

"I discovered that my worst eating binges came immediately following a rejection by my husband. It didn't matter whether he showed signs of dislike or disapproval or simply ignored me, it felt the same to me. I felt lost, angry, and very empty. I felt as if I were starving. And so I ate — and ate and ate!"

My mind was racing. If I substituted the word "flirting" for "eating," "father" for "husband. . . ." That woman ate and ate and ate. I flirted and flirted and flirted. I remembered how lost I felt, how empty . . . *hungry*, just like the writer of this story.

I read the entire article, and then I put the magazine down and leaned back against the pillows, thinking about it, hard.

What was it she had written? "If my own husband wasn't interested in me, found me lacking, then I must be a terrible person, not worth anything."

"If my own father . . . ?"

Could that be it for me too? I *had* felt like that: terrible, ugly, not worth anything.

I scrambled up from the couch and ran up to my room. I tore a blank page from my notebook and found my ball-point pen. For the next two hours, I searched my memories. I tried to remember every detail of my flirting "binges," and I made a list of them in order on the lined paper.

Laura Breen's Gregg
Sandy Bartell's Ronnie
Joanie's Larry
Terri Lannigan's Tommy . . .
The boy at the gas station and, of course, Michael!

It all tallied. Every single incident had happened right after a scene with Daddy. I studied the list and I felt the first prickles of the anger and resentment I was so familiar with now. It *was* all his fault: *He* was the one who had made me do all these terrible things. Why had he pushed me away? Why hadn't he paid more attention to me? Was it really because of the job at S-M?

The anger left me as I thought of all the years Daddy had made me feel special, pretty, worthwhile. For my entire life, right up until last year, I felt fine, totally secure and approved of.

Now it would be good again, just like it used to be. Daddy showed definite signs of becoming his old self, a nice, fun-loving, easygoing husband and father. The question was, could *I*? After all the damage I had done? I wasn't sure if my story would have a happy ending like the woman who had lost over a hundred pounds.

I was surprised when I noticed the time on my clock-radio: four-twenty. Mom and Daddy would be home soon. I hid the list under the blotter on my desk. It was definitely something I didn't want anyone to see.

It occurred to me that I might be all wrong, that I was clutching onto someone else's reasons, someone else's solution. Still, it all *felt* right. But it worried me. If I told anyone about it, would they think I was weird? Was it very abnormal to be so hung up on what my father thought of me? I yearned suddenly for a friend, someone to talk it over with. I missed Debbie so much. And I thought of Terri too; she had always seemed to have the answers to questions long before the rest of us did.

In my room I paced back and forth, and then, too impatient to stay there, I ran downstairs and stood in front of the big living room window.

"Come home," I whispered into the paisley drapes. "Come home now, family, I *need* you."

When they did come home, twenty minutes later, laden with Ferber's boxes and bags, Mom hung up her coat, kicked off her shoes, and headed for the stairs.

"I'm *exhausted*," she said happily. "My feet are killing me. Even my toenails hurt."

She paused on the third step. "I'm going to take a very long, very hot bath. If you don't hear anything after thirty minutes, knock. The way I feel, I may fall asleep and drown."

Daddy made a face at her. "*You're* tired? I'm the one who tried on fifty suits. Susan, I swear I spent the entire day in the dressing room."

Mom laughed. "And your father thought shopping was easy, just a diversion for women who have nothing better to do. Now he knows shopping is a *skill*, maybe even an art, not to mention hard work."

She smiled and continued up the stairs.

"Bill, don't forget my Egg Foo Young," she called over her shoulder. "I'm hungry too."

Daddy groaned.

"She talked me into picking up Chinese food for supper. Which means I have to get back in the car and fight the traffic on Route 18 again. Want to take a ride with me, Susan?"

"Sure," I said quickly. "Just let me get some shoes on."

It had been a long time since Daddy had asked for my company. The same thing occurred to him because he said, "How long has it been since we've taken a ride? I mean, just you and me?"

"A long time. About a year," I said.

I felt, rather than saw him glance at me.

"That long?" He sounded sad and rather sheepish.

It was amazing. In just a few days, Daddy had stopped being a grouchy, unapproachable stranger, and was completely Daddy again. I felt completely comfortable with him now. I could say anything I wanted to.

"It's been terrible, Daddy. I missed you. I thought . . ."

"What did you think, Suse?" I could tell he really wanted to know.

"I thought . . . you *hated* me."

There was a silence, and then he took one hand off the steering wheel and squeezed my shoulder.

"Your mother said the same thing. I made her feel like that too." He sighed. "I don't know. I think back on the past year and it seems unreal, like a nightmare. And I feel now as if I just woke up. I think, was that me?"

"Daddy, it messed me up. I did some awful things because I thought you didn't love me anymore."

We had pulled into the parking lot behind the Fortune Cookie. Daddy parked the car and shut off the motor and lights. He turned in his seat to face me.

"What happened, Suse?" he asked quietly.

Suddenly I was pouring it all out, how flirting had stopped being a natural, lighthearted way of talking to boys. How it had become such a desperate thing, how it had caused me to lose all my friends. I told him all about Debbie and Michael and John. I also told him about the lady who, when she got to know herself, didn't have to be fat anymore. About how I had felt the same way she did.

I was afraid I would cry so I put my fists over my eyes to keep back the tears. I stayed that way while I asked him the question.

"Am I normal?" I asked. "Is it supposed to

matter so much if you like me? Is there something wrong with me?"

His laughter shocked me.

"Oh, honey, I'm not laughing at *you*. It's just that I'm so relieved. You said you did awful things, but what you did, how you acted, is understandable. It's normal for a girl to want and need her father's affection and approval. After all, isn't a girl's father the first important man in her life? The image she has of herself is determined, at least partly, by the image she sees reflected in his eyes. If the image she sees is a good one, well, she will be happy with herself, and be able to have good relationships with the males who come after."

He chuckled. "Wow! Do I sound like an expert or what? I'm impressing myself with this speech. But listen, I'm sure none of it was funny to you and I am sorry, very very sorry. The truth is, I was not thinking about you or your mother. I was only thinking about myself.

"We can't spend the rest of our lives dwelling on our past mistakes and failures. Your mother said that to me. She said, 'Forget about what has been. Let's work on what's happening now and what's going to be.' Nice lady, your mother."

"I guess I thought it was my fault. You had loved me before, I knew that. But had I become someone you didn't like? I kept thinking *I* had changed. I thought I had disappointed you in some way, Daddy."

He took my hands in his and held them tight.

"Take my word for it now that I'm thinking straight again. I love you. You are the best, the nicest, the prettiest girl in the whole world. And far from disappointing me as you grow older, you improve with age, like cheese or wine."

He really was Daddy again, unable to resist a joke. I had to smile.

"You haven't lost anything, Daddy," I said, "But I have. It's too late for me. Debbie and John — I've lost them."

"I'm not sure about that," he said. "How about trying again?"

"Uh unh," I said, shaking my head. "Debbie was definite. She never wants to see me again. And John, well, John is stubborn."

"I'm not saying it will be easy. You may have to work very hard at getting them both to listen. But if you were good friends, then you can be again. Admit you were wrong, tell them you need them. Explain it. Say you're sorry."

"But I was *terrible*," I said. "Sneaky and terrible. How can they forgive me?"

"Have you forgiven me, Suse?" he asked softly.

"Oh, sure," I said. "Now that I understand better."

He squeezed my hands. "That's my girl," he said happily. "Now think about what you just said. You forgive me because now you understand. Isn't it possible Debbie and John will be able to say that too?"

"I don't know . . ." I said doubtfully. "I hurt them a lot."

"At least give them another chance. Will you do that, honey?"

"I'll think about it, Daddy," I said. "I really will."

"Okay," he said briskly and gave me my hands back. "Now let's go in and get the Egg Foo Young before it becomes Egg Foo Old. Then we better get ourselves home and rescue your mother. You don't supposed she's drowned, do you?"

"No," I said, and giggled. "But if she's still in the tub, she'll be pretty darned wrinkled by now."

CHAPTER FOURTEEN

Dad went to bed shortly after ten o'clock. Happily. It was his night off from S-M.

"Just think," he told us, "after May third, I'll be able to sleep every night like a real person."

"I think you should know, Bill," Mom said, trying to hide a smile, "*real* people sometimes stay up *after* ten o'clock, and *real* people often take their wives *out* on a Saturday night."

Dad looked hurt.

"Sheila! You said you were tired. You wanted to stay home and have Chinese food."

Mom was across the room in a second.

"Only kidding, luv," she said, winding her arms around his neck and smiling up at him. "I had a marvelous day. Now go on up to bed and don't worry about us. We're fine."

We were fine; I felt just as good as she did. But why hadn't I noticed it before, I wondered, watching Mom. She was a flirt too. Unlike me, though, she did it best when she was happy.

We made tea, opened a new box of Fig Newtons, and brought our refreshments into the living room. Mom propped herself at one end of the couch, and I settled myself at the other end.

We arranged the afghan cozily over our legs, and as soon as it was safe, Puddy jumped up and arranged her sleek black body between us. It was like old times.

"Ah, I did love this day," Mom said, sighing contentedly. "It reaffirms my belief in miracles."

"I know what you mean," I said. "Everything has changed, and so suddenly."

"It does seem that way, doesn't it?" she said. "I wanted to tell you but I was half afraid your father wouldn't get the job. Didn't want to get your hopes up if it didn't work out."

She made a face and sighed. "I don't know if I could have stood it much longer."

I nodded. She knew *I* knew what she meant.

"Bad year," she said.

"Bad year," I agreed.

"A miracle," she said.

"Magic," I said. "Maybe you're a witch?"

She laughed. "A *good* witch, I hope."

I felt depressed all of a sudden. A witch. The Wicked Witch of the West. Me. She must have noticed my glum look because she reached down and tweaked my big toe through the covers.

"What is it, Susan Bee? I may have been a terrible, neglectful mother all these months, but I'm here for you now."

There was no longer any anger in me, just sadness. I understood that she had survived the past year in the only way she could; lying low, exercising patience, keeping her problems to herself.

But the "Susan Bee" got to me. I felt my eyes fill with tears.

"No Susan B. Anthony anymore, Mom," I said. "John broke up with me."

I saw a flash of sympathy in her eyes.

"I knew something was wrong. And I haven't seen Debbie around either. Oh, Susan, and you didn't even have me."

Now there were tears in her eyes too.

"*She* was there," I said, pointing to Puddy, trying to smile. I didn't want her to feel guilty.

I told her everything. She waited until I stopped talking and then she laid her head back against the couch pillow and stared at the ceiling.

"We all got pretty desperate, didn't we, Susan?"

Then she picked up her head and looked me straight in the eye.

"You've got to talk to Debbie again, and soon. You can't lose her. Maybe John can't understand it, but Debbie will. She'll know what you mean. She's a girl too."

"Oh, Mom," I said. "I wish you were right. I miss her. I know she's just as unhappy as I am about what happened. I'd give anything to make it up to her."

"You have to try. You and I both know now that things can be changed. Nothing is hopeless. If I wanted to count up all my mistakes this year, my regrets, number one would be not facing up to what was happening sooner, letting it drag on for so long. Fortunately both your father and I were able to snap out of it. We can be real people again."

"The kind who stay up after ten o'clock?" I asked teasingly.

She grinned.

"Time, shmime," she said. "Feel like staying up, Susan? Maybe watch the late show?"

"That's the trouble with you, Mom. When you finally decide to pay attention to me, you overdo it. I'm tired. Talking to Dad and then you, my tongue hurts."

Sunday was so warm, so beautiful, I was tempted to put on shorts and a brief top, get out the beach chair, and soak up some sun. Mom and Daddy were already outside, sitting at the red-wood picnic table, drinking coffee and sharing *The New York Times* and *The Home News*. It was a real preview of summer, Bond family style.

But I had something important to do. Mom was right, Daddy too. I had to talk to Debbie. At least I had to *try*.

Mrs. Gilmore was taking advantage of the weather too. She was raking all the rotted leaves and debris from beneath the bushes on the side of their house. In jeans, sneakers, and a red checkered shirt, she looked very young, maybe because she's so tiny.

But up close she didn't look very young, she looked worried. I guess I expected her to be cool to me, even hostile. I wouldn't have been a bit surprised if she had said, "Go home, Susan, haven't you caused enough trouble?"

She didn't. She surprised me more by grasping my hand and pulling me toward a sheltered corner toward the rear of the house.

"I'm so glad you came, Susan. I hoped you

would, but if you hadn't, by the end of the week, I was going to call you."

She sighed. "I'm going to put you on the spot. I *have* to know what's going on. I just cannot stand by and watch my child do this to herself, ruin everything she's accomplished. She won't tell me anything. I can't stand it. I want to help her."

"Is she all right, Mrs. Gilmore?" I dreaded her reply. I had hoped she'd confided in her mother — or someone. I hated to think of Debbie having no one to talk to.

"Oh, she's *all right*," she said, and I thought she sounded angry. "She gets up in the morning and goes to school. She helps around the house the way she always did, she plays Yahtzee with Steve, she does her homework, she eats well . . ."

Suddenly Mrs. Gilmore put her hands up to her face, and pressed her fingertips against her eyelids.

"Susan, she's *eating*! So much eating again. She's *stuffing* herself. And this time, it's not my fault. I beg her not to."

She took her hands away and looked at me.

"Susan, I know whatever happened has something to do with you. I know Debbie is angry with you. When I mentioned your name, she said, 'Mom, I don't ever want to hear her name again.' But she won't explain. Oh, I just want to shake that girl."

I couldn't hide my confusion anymore.

"Mrs. Gilmore, why are you mad at Debbie? You should be mad at me but not at Debbie."

"Maybe," she said. "But what could be so

terrible that she's willing to give up everything she worked for, that you both worked for. It seems like spite to me. I never thought my Debbie was a spiteful person. And I wonder, Susan, just who is she trying to get back at — herself or you or me?"

"Susan, whatever is wrong between you and Debbie, go and talk to her again. Try to straighten things out. I don't want to see her throw away the special years ahead by being fat and friendless again."

She put her arm around my shoulders and she walked me toward the back door.

"I'll go see Debbie now," I said.

Her face clouded.

"I went in the house just before you came. Do you know what she's doing? She's making pudding — a *double* batch. I suspect she plans to eat it all by herself."

"Oh, *boy*! That's just great," I said, suddenly angry.

Debbie was really doing it to herself. And I knew at that moment that I wasn't going to let her. Even if it meant she would hate me for the rest of my life. She was *not* going to eat that pudding. She was *not* going to wear a stupid rubber band around her hair.

CHAPTER FIFTEEN

"You really do want to be a tapioca-face, don't you, Debbie?"

It was our old joke but I said it to shock her, to show her that I knew exactly what she was doing. She had been shocked when I walked in through the back door, pulled out a kitchen chair, and sat down. For a long moment, she stood in front of the stove staring at me, forgetting to stir, the wooden spoon motionless in her hand.

"Get out," she said finally, turning so her back was toward me.

"Not me," I said. "I love tapioca, remember? And judging from the size of that pot, there'll be more than enough for me."

"*Susan*," she said with a warning in her voice.

I steeled myself for a battle; I would have to be hard.

"If you eat all of that by yourself, you'll get fat again and if you won't give me my half, I'll just stay slim and gorgeous."

She didn't answer me but I knew by the way her body stiffened I had gotten to her.

She whirled around suddenly and glared at me.

"I don't want to hear it," she said furiously. "I'm not interested in what you think. I was stupid to think you were my friend, that's all. Now leave me alone."

I didn't move.

"Leave you alone? Why? So you can get to work on becoming the old Debbie Gilmore? How can you go back to that? Why do you want to?"

She didn't answer.

"It's a way of paying me back, isn't it? Show me that anything we did together didn't matter; it was all for nothing. Look at your hair, Debbie. You're deliberately making yourself ugly."

"Who cares?" she spat at me.

"*I* care," I said firmly. "Where's your spirit anyway? You don't have to like me but you do have to like yourself."

She stared at me. "Susan, I don't know where you get your nerve, I really don't."

"Well, I owe it to you," I said slowly. "A lot of things have changed in my life and I'd like to talk to you about it. I want to explain it to you. Maybe you'll be able to understand what happened then."

Now, I guess, I was really pleading with her.

"Will you listen, Debbie? If, when I finish, you still hate me, I will go home and leave you alone."

I could sense her indecision so I tried to lighten things up a little.

"Then you can have all the tapioca to yourself. . . ."

She didn't crack a smile but the word tapioca reminded her. She turned back to the stove, began to stir, and then with a series of quick motions, she dropped the dripping spoon in the sink, turned off the gas burner, and crossed the room to face me. Her face was red.

"Now see what you made me do," she hissed. "It's burned on the bottom, good for nothing. You ruin everything, Susan."

I stood up and pulled out another chair, and pushed her, none too gently, into it.

"It might sound absolutely crazy but my mother said she thought you would understand all this. Because you are a girl and because once you were my friend."

She was looking down at the table and as I watched, a single tear slipped down her cheek and into the corner of her mouth.

"How can I understand you when I don't understand myself?"

She spoke very softly and her voice was breaking.

"I don't know who I am or who I want to be. Part of me wants my old life back because it was . . . safer."

And then her head was down on the kitchen table and she was sobbing.

"I don't want to be pretty anymore. It hurts. *You* hurt."

I laid my hand on her head, on the ridiculously tight ponytail.

"I know I hurt you, Debbie. I know, Deb, it wasn't fair. . . ."

I wanted to cry too but instead I kept talking, and stroking her hair, the way you'd do with a little kid or maybe a pet you loved a lot, like

Puddy. I wanted to pull off that rubber band, and let her hair free, but I didn't. She would have to do that for herself.

"John broke up with me; did you know that? I hurt him too. I can't blame him for being disgusted with me, for not understanding or even trying to. I never told John about any of the things that were bothering me, and I never really told you either. You and John, you both thought I was wonderful, that I could handle everything. He thought it was great that so many boys were interested in me. I think it made him proud. He never dreamed I ever had to do anything to get all that attention. And you thought. . . Well, you both just saw what you wanted to see."

Her head was still down but she appeared to be listening. At least she had stopped crying.

"It was a bad year for me, Deb . . ."

I told her about it, starting even further back than I had with Daddy or Mom. I told her that it is just as hard to have admiration and love from the beginning and have it torn away, as to not ever have it. I told her how I used flattery and smiles and even lies to get the attention I needed so much.

"Not that I really liked Gregg or Ronnie or Larry — or Michael."

I told her all the little details, and about the feelings that were too big for me to handle. I told her how much I had hurt inside.

Finally I ran out of words. I waited for her to answer me, say something, *anything*.

It was hard to talk for so long to someone without any response at all.

"Poor Michael," I said to break the silence. "He's the one I feel sorry for. Remember he told us how lonely he was? He met you and things looked better. Then I got hold of him and confused the daylights out of him."

I ran dry then. There was nothing else to say. I was beginning to feel very uncomfortable, *stupid*. Why didn't she say something?

I looked at her. Her head was in her arms and she wasn't moving. She wouldn't even turn her head toward me again. I thought of all the fun we had together and realized it was never going to be that way for us again. She wasn't going to forgive me.

"One more thing, Debbie," I said, fighting the huge lump in my throat, "I miss you. I need you to talk to, to share stuff with, to call on the phone, and to laugh with . . ."

. I very nearly choked on the next words out of my mouth.

". . . because I'm so lonesome without you."

I couldn't stand it anymore. She hadn't even lifted her head.

"I'll go now . . ." I knew I sounded frantic.

I pushed back the chair and ran past her, out the door. You're a fool, Susan Bond, I thought wildly. You were honestly you for a change and she didn't understand or care. She just . . . sat there.

I was out in the bright sunshine, running, running, because I was hurting so much again. No, not again. It hadn't hurt quite this bad before.

"Darn you, Debbie Gilmore," I said out loud as I ran.

I caught a glimpse of Mrs. Gilmore as I ran past the side of their house. She looked startled and then, worried again.

By the time I got home, I was much calmer. Calm enough to sit quietly in my room and think about it.

I had been a fool about a lot of things. Had I really thought just by talking my brains out all weekend, spreading out my insides like cheese on crackers, I could solve everything? Make everything all right again?

Sitting there, I looked idly around my room, noticing that my closet was really a disaster. Fine, I thought, it will be something for me to do with the rest of the day.

Then something happened. I began to compare the cleaning of my closet to what I had been trying to do with my life.

When you clean a closet, first take all the ugly stuff out, the stuff that you hate and put it in a pile. Throw-aways, garbage. But the other pile, the good things, you hang up again, neatly, and as you do, you check to see if anything needs repairing; buttons to be sewed back on, a hem to fix. If so, you fix them. At the end, when the closet is neat-perfect, you feel satisfied with yourself. It's a job well done. You feel good because your closet has been a disaster area for a very long time.

That's what I had tried to do, with Mom and Daddy and with Debbie: get rid of everything ugly and try to repair and save the nice things. But it didn't work. A closet was a closet and my life was my life and it was still a disaster. I didn't know what else I could do to fix it.

I suppose the pain had been worse today because I had believed what Mom said: Debbie would understand. Well, I just better forget it with Debbie, I thought. I can't say anything to change her mind about me. Could I start over somehow? At school? Could I make other friends? I didn't know that but I did know one thing: it wasn't going to be easy. As I said to Debbie, I had earned myself a reputation.

I was so tired of thinking about it. No more today, I decided. Tomorrow, maybe.

My parents were so happy doing their pre-summer thing, I didn't have the heart to put a damper on their good spirits by talking about what had happened at Debbie's. So I joined them outside, and started doing what they were doing; getting things set up for an early Sunday dinner — outdoors.

"Love cookouts," I said as cheerily as I could. "I hope you made your potato salad, Mom. You can't have a cookout without that."

"All done," she said. "While you were gone. It's in the fridge chilling now. Plus *steaks*! Big shot executives and their families must eat well."

"Big shot executives and their families must get the fire going before they *can* eat steak," Daddy said. "Sheila, you do the thing with the charcoal, okay? It always fizzles out on me."

That was the way it went — light stuff, family stuff. The hurt had eased enough so I could eat and talk and even smile without being too phony about it. I hoped they wouldn't ask me about Debbie. I wasn't ready to talk about it yet. I yearned for John and remembered all the cook-outs we'd shared.

Mom was pouring a second cup of coffee, and it was beginning to get dark, when suddenly she gasped.

"Omigosh, Susan, I almost forgot. Mrs. Pulaski called when I was in the house before. She wants you to come over for a minute. I told her you would. And then I promptly forgot it. Why don't you run over there right now, Susan. Daddy and I will put this stuff away."

"Sure," I said. Why not? Except for my parents, Mrs. Pulaski was the only friend I had left.

"Be back soon," I said, taking one last bite of potato salad. "But not *too* soon," I rolled my eyes at them and pointed.

They were holding hands and Mom's head was resting on Daddy's shoulder.

CHAPTER SIXTEEN

Walking over to the Pulaski's house in the deepening dusk, I felt almost peaceful. Not peaceful-happy but at least I was quiet inside, resigned.

I knocked on the door and made a mental promise not to cry on Mrs. Pulaski's shoulder. If she had called me, then she must really need someone to talk to, someone to cheer her up. She rarely called, and never asked for anything. She would rather die, I knew, than be thought of as a pest.

When she opened the door, I had a smile ready, as well as a hug. I wasn't prepared for her wide smile, though, or the look of happy excitement on her face. Her faded blue eyes were twinkling behind her glasses.

"Ah, Susan, come in. We were waiting."

I glanced toward Mr. Pulaski. He was far away in television land; he didn't even know I was there. I wanted to tell her she didn't have to pretend, to say "we."

"We see you eating the barbecue," she said gaily. "It is like summer, no? I tell your mama, tell Susan we want her."

I just smiled and let her lead me to the kitchen. Now I understood. Katya, not Mr. Pulaski, had been the other part of "we."

"What's new with Katya?" I asked politely. Probably that's why she looked so excited; the bird had probably mastered some new trick.

"Did Katya . . ."

The words stuck in my throat, and I stopped short. Debbie was sitting at Mrs. Pulaski's kitchen table, a cup of tea raised to her lips. But the cup didn't quite hide the corners of her mouth; she was *smiling*.

She looked beautiful. Her hair was freshly washed, falling in soft waves around her face. She had done makeup too (maybe too much blush, or was that a *real* blush?) She did look shy and unsure of herself. I stood there staring, not moving.

Then she put her cup down and pointed toward it.

"No sugar, I'll have you know, just lemon."

I opened my mouth but words wouldn't come.

"Mrs. Pulaski said if I put baking soda in the tapioca pan and left it overnight, all the burned gunk would come right up."

"No kidding," I said weakly.

She lowered her eyes, and her mouth turned down in an exaggerated, sad face.

"I'm so sorry, Susan, I couldn't save any of the tapioca for you. But if you want me to, I'll make another batch, just for you. You really do need some fattening up. Besides, it's not fair for you to be the only slim, gorgeous one."

Then, in one quick move, I was beside her.

She stood up and we were hugging each other, laughing and crying at the same time.

"Debbie," I croaked.

"Oh, Susan," she crooned.

"How come . . .?" I began.

"Just shush," she said, giggling against my shoulder. "And get your eyes out of my hair. You're getting it all wet."

We pulled away and looked at each other hard and laughed. I could tell she was just as happy as I was, and just as flustered. All this emotion was getting to us.

We both noticed Mrs. Pulaski at the same time. She was standing off to one side of the kitchen. She had her hands clasped, resting on her bosom, and her head was cocked toward her shoulder; her eyes were dreaming, dreaming.

"Mrs. Pulaski," I said gently, "come sit with us now."

She didn't move, but a tender little smile played over her lips.

"I had friend like that," she said softly. "Marya. In the old country."

She snapped out of her reverie.

"Long time ago."

Then she put her own memories aside. "My heart is glad. You make up your" — she searched for a word — "your *gobbles*?"

Debbie and I exchanged glances. "I think she means quarrel," I said.

After that, I was in no hurry to get home. As I had cleaned out my imaginary closet, I felt now that all the old, ugly stuff had been thrown away, and Debbie and I, our friendship, was repaired, almost like new.

But not quite. I filled her in on the SUPER-BALL progress, assuming she would start working with me again the next day.

"Decorations are almost all done and tickets sales are great. Guess everyone wants to be a superhero," I said.

Debbie put her elbow on the table and rested her chin in her hand. She looked glum.

"Do you even care about the dance now, Susan? I don't think I do. Now, neither of us will be going."

Suddenly I felt glum too. It would always be there between us, the reason why we weren't going — *me*!

I guess she noticed my expression because she said, "Hey, now don't get all depressed. I don't care anymore *why* we're not going. What's done is done. It just doesn't matter to me much now whether tickets are selling, or it's a success."

She looked at me. "You know, Susan, maybe *you* could still go. If you talked to John again . . ."

"No," I said firmly. "I wouldn't have the nerve for *that*, and besides, I told you, John is stubborn as a mule."

"I still think you could try," she said, and smiled mischievously. "And with your *talents*, I also think you could win him over. No one's going to get *mad* at you if you flirt with John, you know."

I made a face and changed the subject. "Why don't you talk to Michael? I bet he'd jump at a second chance."

She shook her head vigorously. "Uh *unh*, I wouldn't *dare*!"

Mrs. Pulaski had been sitting quietly as we talked, but her fingers holding knitting needles and wool were flying. Now she put her work down and made a clearing sound in her throat. She looked first at Debbie and then at me.

"I have idea," she said shyly.

"What?" I asked eagerly. "All ideas will be gratefully accepted."

"Susan, you are afraid to talk with your boy, John, yes?"

"Yes!" I said emphatically. "It just wouldn't do any good."

"And you, Debbie, you are afraid to talk to Michael, yes?"

"Yes," Debbie said. "You're absolutely right, Mrs. Pulaski."

"Then you do this . . ." She hesitated and I detected a twinkle in her eyes. "Debbie will talk to John and Susan will talk to Michael. You do good deed for each other. Friends do that, no?"

"No!" I said.

"You mean 'yes,' dopey," Debbie said.

"Yes," I said. "I get confused."

"I'm game if you are," Debbie said. "I'm not afraid of John. I'd feel okay talking to him. I wouldn't be asking for myself, you know what I mean, Susan? It wouldn't be like begging."

"I do know what you mean," I said. "Besides, I would like to straighten things out with Michael too. I feel really bad about what I did to him. I think he might believe me as long as I stick to the subject of Debbie Gilmore."

146

I smiled at her. "Girl Scout honor."

She gave me a quizzical look. "I didn't know you were a Girl Scout, Susan."

"I'm not," I admitted. "But *still* . . ."

"It's a good idea, Mrs. Pulaski. Thank you."

"Mmmm," Debbie grinned. "Good idea, *if* it works."

But Mrs. Pulaski wasn't through, she had another good idea or rather, a gift for us.

"If you go to dance, I make nice costume for you each." She lowered her eyelids modestly. "I sew pretty good."

I laughed. "*Pretty good?* You sew beautifully. She really does, Deb. You should see some of the things she's made."

"But maybe not the plastic spider costume," Mrs. Pulaski said anxiously. "Something with pretty color, maybe?"

"Definitely," Debbie said. "If by some miracle I do get to go to the dance, I want to look *pretty*. No spider lady for me."

We stayed so long at Mrs. Pulaski's, Mom finally called to make sure I was there.

"Mom, Debbie's here."

That was all the explanation I needed to give. I knew she would understand immediately. She did.

"Oh, *great!*" she said, "I knew she would . . ."

I interrupted her, laughing. "I know, you're dying to say it, aren't you? *I told you so?*"

She laughed too. "Well, I did! Just don't be too late, okay? It's a school night."

But just before she hung up, she half-whispered, "Have fun. I'm *so* glad for you."

When I got off the phone, I noticed Debbie's faint smile. I realized she knew exactly what I had been talking about.

"My mother has complete faith in you, Deb," I said.

"My mother feels the same about you," she said. "I had a long talk with her after you left."

Maybe we would have pursued the subject, but at that moment, Mr. Pulaski shuffled into the kitchen, brown felt slippers flopping around his skinny ankles. He stood there for a moment blinking at us, as if the bright kitchen and *we* were too much for him. For that minute, I had the thought that he was feeling kind of lost and bewildered.

"Sophie," he said, squinting at her, his neck thrust forward. "Sophie, the television is over."

It was as if he were asking her, "What shall I do now?"

"Okay," she said cheerfully. "We will have our tea and talk now."

She put her knitting in a plastic bag and tucked it away on the shelf behind her. She smiled at us.

"We talk at night, you see," she said, a little apologetic smile on her face. "Stanley, he tells me what he sees on the television and in the town. My Stanley, he is the good story-teller."

She smiled at him fondly and his pinched face relaxed.

"Good night to you, girls," she said as we stood up to leave. "I am happy for you."

"Thank you for everything, Mrs. Pulaski," I said.

"For everything," Debbie echoed.

And then the most amazing thing happened. Mr. Pulaski almost ran for the chair I had just vacated, and slid into it eagerly. He put both bony elbows on the table, and rested his head in his hands and gazed intently across the table at his wife.

I had *never, never* seen him look at Mrs. Pulaski like that in my life. He was looking at her as if she were the most beautiful, the most interesting, the most wonderful woman in the world. And, of course, she *is*.

But can you believe that? *Mr. Pulaski?*

CHAPTER SEVENTEEN

Before we parted, Debbie and I agreed to do the John-Michael Peace Talks right away. The dance was two weeks from Friday, she reminded me.

"And Mrs. Pulaski needs all the time she can get for the costumes," I added.

Debbie frowned. "We haven't even decided who to be."

"First things first," I told her. "Let's see if we're even going."

I told Debbie what time John usually got home from work.

"Call him about six-thirty. If you call him any later, he'll probably be asleep."

I knew from experience John was apt to come home, eat supper, and conk out. All the fresh air and the hard, physical work made him very sleepy.

We decided I'd get to Michael right after school.

"I'll chase him home if I have to," I said, adding, "I'll probably have to. When he sees me, he'll run."

150

"Call me right after you talk to him," Debbie said. "I'll be *dying*."

Then she held up two crossed fingers. "Wish me luck, Susan. With John. I don't have any experience talking to boys, you know."

"You'll do fine," I said. "I'm not worried about you."

But I *was* worried about John. I really didn't have too much hope no matter how persuasive Debbie was. But it was worth a try. I wanted her to try.

By four-thirty Monday afternoon I picked up the phone and called Debbie.

"I think you'd make a fantastic Wonder Woman," I said matter-of-factly.

"Oh, *sure*," she said and then screamed. "*What? Tell me!*"

"All I'm going to tell you right now is that you better not hang on the phone with me. Michael is probably trying to call you right now. His mother needed something at the store but he said as soon as he got home, he'd call you. That would be . . ." I paused for effect. ". . . about *now*."

"Oh-hhh," she said.

"It's all set," I said briskly. "You don't have to worry about a thing. Michael is overjoyed. He said he had been very depressed about the whole thing."

"Was he still . . ."

"Mad at me? Nah, he forgives me. But I can tell you, he's cautious with me, ver-y cautious. Anyway, he's going to ask you to the dance. Now get off the phone!"

151

"Oh, Susan, thank you," she said. "I wasn't sure . . ."

"Well, be sure now. And Debbie, call me, after you talk to John, I mean."

"Don't worry," she said. "I will. And it's going to work out for you too, you'll see. I'm sure of it."

I was glad she was because I certainly wasn't. Not sure at all.

I very nearly broke my neck racing for the phone. I hadn't noticed Puddy sleeping on the floor beside my desk and I tripped over her. I couldn't get my balance and I just kept on going out of control, until Daddy reached out and caught me.

"Whoa," he said. "Take it easy. The phone isn't that important, is it?"

"Yes," I yelled, and ran for it. It was quarter of seven; it *had* to be Debbie.

"What?" I said, forgetting to say hello.

She sounded funny. "Well, I'm not sure yet. I called him, but . . ."

I had a sinking sensation, the kind you get when an elevator stops too fast.

"But what, Debbie?" I just knew John didn't want any part of me.

"He couldn't talk on the phone. He said his Dad was expecting an important call."

Hope returned. "Oh, so he's going to call you back?"

"Not exactly," she said. "He's coming over."

I was startled. "He's coming over your house?

I thought about it for a few seconds. "He is willing to talk about me, though, isn't he, Deb?"

I wanted her to tell me everything he said, word for word. I figured I would be able to read between the lines better than Debbie could.

But, the way she told me, he hadn't said much.

"Actually, Susan, I didn't really get a chance to say *why* I was calling. I just said I wanted to talk to him about something."

Her voice trailed off and I couldn't think of anything to say to fill the silence.

"I'm so nervous," she said finally. "I mean, I didn't think I'd have to do this face to face."

"What time did he say he'd be over?" I asked slowly.

Something terrible was happening to me. My hands were cold, and my stomach felt all queer and queasy.

"In about fifteen minutes. He said we could go for a Coke at Fritzie's and talk there." She hesitated. "It's not what we planned. Susan, it's all right if I go, isn't it? I mean, do you mind?"

"Of course I don't mind," I said quickly. "Why should I mind? You're helping me."

Are you, Debbie, I wondered silently and then immediately hated myself for what I was thinking.

"Anyway, you better get off the phone and get ready. Good luck," I said as casually as I could.

"Okay," she said. "I'll call you later."

Did she sound too happy and excited about

going to Fritzie's with John? Or was that just my imagination?

Of course it was. I was just being stupid.

I went back to my desk and picked up my math book. I spent the next few minutes finding page 81, a piece of paper, sharpening some pencils, unwrapping a stick of gum. I *was* going to do my homework. I *wasn't* going to think about anything else.

Okay. Start. Do problems one through nine.

The black and white of the page blurred into gray.

Problem one: Fritzie's plus John plus Debbie equals Together.

I shook my head impatiently. No. I was not going to think about that. The page came back into focus.

Problem one. John hadn't known Debbie wanted to talk about me so I wasn't the reason he was rushing over to her house, taking her out, so that meant . . .

It doesn't mean anything, Susan, I told myself sternly. *Don't be a dope.*

He said he'd pick her up in fifteen minutes? He sure wasn't wasting any time.

Stop it.

Had Mr. Anthony really been expecting a call? Or was that John's way of getting to see Debbie, to take her to Fritzie's?

No, Susan.

Everyone would see them together. I could just hear Joanie Sangerville. "Look who's here. Serves Susan Bond right."

I slammed the math book shut.

Problems one through nine.

Susan is jealous. Susan is scared. Susan is worried. Etcetera, etcetera. Serves Susan right.

I got up and went over to my bed. I wanted to just lie down, pull the covers over me, and go to sleep. No more thoughts. I would tell Mom to wake me up when Debbie called. Then I would know once and for all. Success for me or failure; John or no John.

But I knew I couldn't sleep.

I guess it's really true what people say, that we are our own worst enemies. Tonight I sure was. I was really doing a job on myself. And why? Just because I had been untrustworthy with other girls' boyfriends, did I expect Debbie to be? I couldn't blame John one bit if he did decide to ask Debbie out. It wouldn't be her fault. And even if she did decide to go out with him . . .

No. She wouldn't. I *knew* she wouldn't.

But it would be the perfect revenge, wouldn't it, Susan?

Then I was ashamed of myself, really ashamed. Debbie did not want revenge. She was my friend and I knew that for sure.

And whether John still liked me or not, he never would do anything just to get back at me. I knew he wouldn't deliberately hurt anyone. John had always been, and was still, a good guy.

I went back to my desk again and opened my book to page 81. But just before I really got down to work, I had one last thought: Now you know how they all felt: Laura, Sandy, Joanie,

Terri. And Debbie. Now you know how awful it was for them.

Do problems one through nine. I picked up my pencil and began.

CHAPTER EIGHTEEN

By the time I finished my math, worked on vocabulary, and read two chapters in my American History book, it was only nine-thirty. *Only.* Where was Debbie? Why hadn't she called?

Daddy was getting ready for work. He had given his notice and this would be his last week at S-M. I could hear him downstairs rejoicing again.

"Friday night I'll be a free man. Think of it, Sheila, *free.*"

But although he was happy now, I noticed he still got grouchy and irritable sometimes.

"Stage fright," Mom said. "New job jitters. Perfectly understandable."

Now I had the jitters too. *Why didn't Debbie call?*

I decided to go downstairs and visit with Daddy for a few minutes; he had to leave at quarter of ten.

Daddy was standing by the window. He had pulled back the drapes and was peering out. He threw me a look over his shoulder.

"What did you do, Suse, tell your boyfriend

to wait till your old man leaves before he comes over?"

He didn't sound angry, just amused more than anything.

"No," I said honestly. "And I don't call you 'my old man' either."

I went over and stood beside him. "Why did you ask me *that*?"

He dropped the curtain, turned to face me, and hooked his thumbs in his belt trying to look like a tough guy. He scowled fiercely.

"Well, he's here, and if *you* don't tell him, *I* will."

I guess my eyes widened. I know my mouth fell open.

". . . that he's *always* welcome."

Daddy was laughing at me. "You should see your face, Suse. You look scared to death."

"*John?*" I whispered. "Is *John* here?"

"Well," he said, "It's John's car, and the guy coming up the path walks like John and he has John's face. I believe it's *John*."

Daddy put his arm around my shoulder.

"If it's of any help to you," he said, "John looks scared to death too."

"Oh, no," I said and ran for the stairs. "I look awful — my hair. Daddy, answer the door, please. I want to fix . . ."

I kept running, not bothering to explain any further, but at the top of the stairs, I turned and called down to Daddy.

"Please," I said, "don't let him get away."

My hand was shaky as I brushed my hair, and

it was difficult to breathe. I crossed my fingers mentally.

"Wish me luck," I said to the mirror. "Let John's coming over be a good sign."

The mirror didn't answer but it didn't lie; I *did* look scared to death.

I could hear their voices: Mom's, Dad's, but not John's. Was he here? Maybe he had changed his mind at the last minute. Maybe he had just given Daddy a message for me. Maybe a note that said something like, "Thanks, Susan, but no thanks."

Then I heard John say, "So long, Mr. Bond. Have a good night."

A moment later, I heard Mom coming upstairs and her bedroom door close. I was on my own. Talk about nervous; my throat was as dry as stale bread, and my knees had a life of their own.

But I couldn't put it off any longer. I had to go downstairs, face him, accept whatever it was he had come to tell me, good *or* bad.

John was kneeling beside the brown chair scratching Puddy's stomach. Puddy was in heaven, purring ecstatically. He didn't look up even though I knew he had heard me come into the room.

"Your Dad seems real happy about his new job. Your Mom too. It's nice to see them smile again."

His voice was low and even. I couldn't tell what kind of mood he was in. But at least he was speaking to me.

"Oh, it is," I said eagerly, glad to have something to talk about. "It's a great opportunity for him, a real challenge, he says."

He still didn't look up.

"Must run in the family," he said very softly. I was puzzled. "What?" I said.

"You like a challenge too, don't you, Susan?"

Oh. So he *was* here to be nasty, to rub it in. I wouldn't have believed it of him. I didn't answer. What could I say?

He looked up at me now, looked me straight in the eye. He wasn't smiling.

"I've got a challenge for you, Susan. If you want, you can start on it right now."

"What are you talking about," I said. I tried to prepare myself. What *was* he up to?

"Talked to your friend Debbie tonight," he said. "For at least two hours. I found out a lot of surprising things about you. Most of it I could believe but there was one thing I just couldn't swallow. I think Debbie exaggerates."

He stood up and walked around the room, not looking at me. He appeared to be thinking about something.

"No, I can't believe it," he said. "You going to have to prove it to me."

I didn't like this at all. He had to be making fun of me.

"Please tell me what this is all about, John," I said quietly. No matter what happened, I was going to keep my dignity.

"Well," he said, "It's like this. Debbie must be prejudiced. She's a real fan of yours, you know."

"What did she say?" I asked cautiously.

"Debbie was certain you could make me change my mind about you. Me, stubborn mule Anthony. She said you had a gift for melting guys' hearts. She wasn't being sarcastic, Susan. I really think she's proud of your . . . *talents*. She doesn't think I can resist you for more than five minutes. I told her that she was wrong. I was really stubborn. No one had ever made me change my mind."

He was standing there, three feet away from me. He put his head back and looked at me from under his eyelashes. I had always loved it when he did that. He looked so . . . *lovable*!

"Think you can do it, Susan? Think you can make me say I love you in five minutes?"

A faint smile appeared on his face. "Bet you can't," he said ever so softly.

I got it then. I didn't know whether to kiss him or hit him.

"John Michael Anthony, you're playing with me. You're just . . ." I couldn't say it.

"Just what, Susan? Just *flirting*?" He laughed. "You're right, I am. How did I do anyway? On a scale of one to ten?"

I had to laugh.

"Ten," I said. "A definite ten. You're better at it than I am."

He took a step toward me. "Five minutes," he said. "Starting *now*."

And then I was in his arms, his warm, strong, wonderful arms, and I was overwhelmed with a sense of joy and relief.

"Oh, John, I missed you so much."

He bent his face toward me and our lips met. It was the best kiss ever. Then he pulled back his head and looked down at me: the eyelash trick again.

"Four minutes," he whispered.

"You're such a wonderful guy, John." I gazed at him adoringly and batted my eyelashes like mad. I even gave my hair a shake so it would brush against his face. "The girl who gets you would be the luckiest girl in the world. So handsome, so . . ."

"Three minutes — you're doing fine."

He was trying hard not to laugh and so was I. It was fun, though, and I didn't want to stop.

"Whenever you look at me, you know, the way you do . . . I just melt . . ."

I decided to lay it on thick. I opened my eyes as wide as I could, gathered all my forces, and made them sparkle at him. At the same time, I smiled so hard, my lips pressed against my teeth and made them itch. I couldn't hold it back anymore; I laughed out loud.

"My teeth itch, John," I said between spasms of laughter. "How can I be flirtatious when my teeth itch?"

He had no mercy.

"Two minutes," he said, still holding me.

I stopped laughing then and kissed him. Not once, but half a dozen times. Quick, soft, little butterfly kisses, and the sixth one — a long, long kiss. When I pulled away finally, we were both breathless.

"One minute," he said weakly.

I didn't know what else to do. I just hugged him tight and whispered his name over and over.

"Thirteen seconds, twelve seconds . . ." he said, letting himself laugh too.

"I love you, Susan. I never really stopped loving you." He grinned at me. "Debbie's smart. She knew what she was talking about."

I pulled away then, and walked away from him. There was something I had to say, and I wouldn't be able to do it properly with his arms around me.

"John, I'm so sorry."

He was beside me in a second.

"Forget it, Susan. It's all behind us now."

His smile was very tender, and I was sure then he really did still love me.

"I want you to do me a favor, though," he said, his eyes glinting.

"Anything!"

"Tell Debbie I was a number ten. She wasn't sure how well I'd do."

"I'll tell her eleven if you want me to," I said. "Or a hundred. You *are* the best, John."

He hugged me very tight.

"That's why I love you, Susan Bee. Besides being pretty, you've got very good taste."

"I know," I said and smiled. I think I was still smiling while he kissed me.

CHAPTER NINETEEN

When John decided he wanted to go to the SUPERBALL as Tarzan, Debbie talked me into going as Sheena, Queen of the Jungle.

"Don't just be Jane," she said. "All she gets to do is sweep out the treehouse while Tarzan and Cheetah have fun swinging around the jungle. As Sheena, you could look really sensational. Do your hair all wild and lion's mane-ish. Buy some tawny makeup."

I have to hand it to her, Debbie certainly learns fast.

Mrs. Pulaski had some misgivings about our costumes. When I brought over the fake leopard fur, and told her what sides to sew up, she frowned and looked very doubtful.

I had some doubts too. Did I really want to look sensational? Wouldn't it be better to be someone low-key like, say, Lois Lane?

But when John and I walked into the dance as Tarzan and Sheena, I have to admit I was proud; I knew we looked terrific. John hadn't needed any makeup to be tawny and tan; he is from working out-of-doors. And with his dark, curly hair, muscles, and leopard fur, he looked so handsome he took my breath away. When he first saw me in *my* costume, all he could do was give one long, drawn-out whistle, and then re-membering who he was, an ear-splitting Tarzan yell.

Which was fine. I wanted *him* to like the way I looked. But mentally, I was making a promise to him: I may *look* like a Queen of the Jungle, but I'm not going to *act* like one. And maybe everyone else would expect me to be Sheena, but they would be wrong; I was going to be *Jane*. No swinging around tonight, and *no flirting*, not ever. From now on, John had nothing to worry about.

Debbie made a beautiful Wonder Woman, I thought, and Michael, a perfect Flash Gordon. In fact, *all* the costumes were so great, and the decorations so stunning, I think the entire first part of the dance was spent with all of us ad-miring everything and everyone.

Everyone was having a wonderful time; the flashing "stars" overhead were only part of the reason why the faces around me seemed to shine.

Except me. I wasn't happy because, though I tried, I couldn't relax. I hung onto John for dear life, kept my eyes down, and my mouth shut. It was safer that way, and besides, I didn't know what else to do. Finally, John noticed.

"What's the matter, Susan? Don't you feel good?" he asked when the band had taken their first rest break.

"I feel fine," I said quickly. "Don't worry about me. I guess I'm just enjoying everything in a quiet way, you know?"

He gave me *that* look. "In a *quiet* way?"

"Yes," I said, not looking at him. "I guess I just feel quiet tonight. Happy, though."

He reached over and took my hand. "Happy, huh? Hands as cold as ice, so uptight you can't even keep time to the music, or look at me. So quiet and peaceful you can't say a word to me, or anyone else. Susan, I repeat, what's wrong?"

For a second, I was really annoyed. What did he want from me? Here I was, trying to be *good*, and he was complaining.

"I'm trying to be what you want," I began, and then had to stop. There was a definite quiver in my voice. Any minute, I knew I was going to cry.

John led me further back into the dim corner.

"Listen to me, Susan. I don't want you to stop being *you*. I understand now that your way of talking, your funny, flirty little ways, the way you smile and flash your eyes, that special way you toss your hair around, all those things are part of the girl I love. As Debbie said, it's a talent. I agree. I like it. I only ask one thing . . ."

He hesitated, and in the dim light, I could see the flash of teeth; he was smiling in a big way.

"While you're my girl, save most of the flirting for me, okay? I mean, the heavy duty stuff. I don't mean you can't look at another guy, or not have fun. But I have found out a couple of things about myself through . . . what happened. Number one, I'm not as stubborn as I thought, and number two, I'm kind of jealous. I guess I always have been. I just kept it hidden. But that's my

166

problem, Susan, not yours. I don't want you to change too much."

I was looking up at him and as he talked I saw that his curls were tangled in the front. I reached up and combed through them with my fingers. As I did, I tilted my head and gave him just the faintest smile.

"Does Tarzan know what a comb is?" I asked ever so softly.

He threw back his head and laughed, and then gave me a huge bear hug, holding me so tightly I couldn't breathe.

"Tarzan no need comb, Tarzan has Sheena."

He let me go then, and stepped back, and let out the most awful ear-splitting yell, pounding his chest like a wild man. I saw everyone turn around and stare at us, but I wasn't one bit embarrassed. I loved it, in fact. And I loved *him*. There was no doubt in my mind about that. The rest of the SUPERBALL was going to be sensational.

And so was I.

The minute I relaxed, the stars began to shine for me too, and everything about the dance seemed to be pure magic. I didn't want to miss a single part of it. I really rushed when I started for the girls' room to comb my hair and fix my lipstick.

"Be right back, John," I said hastily, dashing toward the door. If I hurried I would be back when the music started again.

For the first time, I really felt like Sheena, running through the deserted hall, my hair streaming out behind me. I pushed open the door to the girls' room with more strength than I intended, and it banged hard against the wall.

Terri Lannigan stood there, wide-eyed, her mouth open.

"Oh," she gasped. "You scared me."

"Sorry," I said. "I guess I got carried away."

Now, I *was* embarrassed. I didn't know what to say.

But she did. "I've been wanting to see you. Susan, I've been wondering about something. Tommy asked you out and you said no. Is that true?"

"Yes," I said shortly. "It's true."

Was she going to start trouble now? I didn't want that, not tonight.

"Why didn't you go out with him?" she asked quietly.

"Terri, Tommy is *your* guy," I said patiently. "You two are like gloves, a definite pair. I never wanted to break you up, no matter what anyone believes."

She surprised me by laughing merrily.

"My Dad says Tommy and I are like peanut butter and jelly. I think *I'm* the peanut butter. Some of my ideas seem to stick to the roof of his mouth."

"It's kind of complicated, Terri. I don't really know if I can explain . . ."

Her fine gray eyes were soft.

"I'd like to talk about it, if you do," she said. "Let's get together soon, all right?"

I nodded eagerly. "Sure, it's all right. I'd like that."

We didn't say anything more and I was glad. I could tell she wanted to get back to the dance as much as I did. But before I went back to John, I made a decision. I'd have to be honest with Terri and tell her why I'd acted as I had. Later, maybe, I would be able to square things with Laura and Sandy, even Joanie. I had missed them all.

Yes, I thought, maybe everything would be all right now. And then I laughed out loud. Who was I kidding? Everything was going to be *super*! I just *knew* it. I took a quick final look in the mirror and ran back to John, smiling all the way.